THE ICE AGE

Kirsten Reed was born in 1973 in Seattle. She grew up in New Zealand, in Germany and in various parts of the US before moving to Australia as an adult. She now lives in Brisbane with her partner, two cats and various foster animals, and works as a freelance artist and writer. *The Ice Age* is her first novel.

KIRSTEN REED

THE ICE AGE

PICADOR

First published 2009 by the Text Publishing Company, Melbourne, Australia

First published in Great Britain 2010 by Picador
an imprint of Pan Macmillan, a division of Macmillan Publishers Limited
Pan Macmillan, 20 New Wharf Road, London N1 9RR
Basingstoke and Oxford
Associated companies throughout the world
www.panmacmillan.com

ISBN 978-0-330-51335-7

1 3 5 7 9 8 6 4 2

A CIP catalogue record for this book is available from
the British Library.

Printed by CPI Mackays, ME5 8TD

Visit **www.picador.com** to read more about all our books
and to buy them. You will also find features, author interviews and
news of any author events, and you can sign up for e-newsletters
so that you're always first to hear about our new releases.

For Dan and his fangs

There were those teeth. Those little vampire teeth, glinting sharply as he stared at the road in front of us in a vacant daze. We drove past all the gaudy painted signs telling us where the next doughnut shop was, the nearest hamburger joint; pizza, now doughnuts again. The road was stretched across this wasteland like a big silver rubber band, stapled down by fluorescent mustardy-yellow lines. Even the sky looked tacky, needlessly aqua, a tourist's T-shirt. And that white skin. His iceberg eyes, luminous white-blue, burning into the distance. I wished he would hurry up and bite me. Drain me of this wish, pull me over to the other side. Surely anyone with teeth that sharp…

We stopped at a roadside diner. People asked if I was his daughter. They ask all the time. Hoping, accusing. We never say yes, and we never say no. We ate our food at a booth in a hungry, self-conscious rush, straight out of the wrappers. They didn't have plates. We left a tip, just change. The waitress scooped it up straight away as we slid out of the booth. She was middle-aged and bulgy, in a proper matronly waitress's dress. She shot us what I suppose was intended to be a look of gratitude. She really only managed a weak glare. I guess that's the countryside for you. People are a little edgy.

Of course Gunther's never tried anything on with me. It must be the age difference. He's probably right. I do and don't feel young. I know he's old, and in comparison I'm young. But it's the two of us together, and I must be old beyond my years to be hanging around here with him, talking, reading, smoking, riding around in the car observing stuff. I'm getting it all. I'm starting to get it, that is. He said when he picked me up way back there he thought I looked young, but my intelligence made me look older in the face.

I was cutting across a gas station lot, weaving through the pumps. I hadn't been on the road long.

There were a lot of seedy characters lurking around. Pretty much everyone filling up their cars looked like they'd just been busted out of prison. I was trying to pass through undetected, but the station speaker system was piping out KISS. 'I Was Made for Loving You'. An anthem to fucking if ever there was one, recorded before I was even born. Those songs bring out the animal in some people. I was the only female in sight, so by default the closest thing to a Rock Video Fantasy Chick. Gunther pulled out in his big long tank of a car and I stuck my thumb out. He peered over at me with a kind of worried look, and I got in. He asked where I was headed. I asked where he was headed.

After a brief silence I asked, 'Is there a penitentiary around here, or something?'

He smirked and said, 'No, but there is a meat packing plant.' I figured he must be vegetarian or something.

He said he thought I was about twenty. Which is still too young. But not running-from-the-law young. I guess I'm not worth it. I'm good company so he keeps me around. Sometimes I think anyone would be good company on this stretch of road. I said lucky for him I'm a virgin. Because if they test me, he's in the clear. He said no one would believe he hasn't molested me anyway, so what difference does it make? I said I could tell them I'm a perfectly willing driving companion, and he said, 'Brainwashed…'

Now this is taking a long time to write, because it's hard to type when you're stoned. Gunther bought us this ageing portable typewriter. Really, it's his, but I use it more often. I just like to keep busy. And Gunther says if I have something I want to do, or be, I should start now. He said a painter is someone who gets up in the morning and paints, nearly every day. And writers, by his definition, just write things down, a lot. So far the only thing I've seen him do on a daily basis is drive, and smoke. He smokes and smokes and smokes, rolling joint after joint, in every hotel room we stop in. He always looks so gentlemanly doing it, throughout the entire ritual, in every practised gesture. Cutting out a little card and rolling it between his thumb and index finger, chopping, sprinkling, caressing it all into place. And the licking…I remember his old friend Glorie Wethers. Funny old broad. Gunther's known her from way back.

He introduced us a few weeks back, on a Mississippi steamboat of all places. At an art opening.

She'd lent one of Gunther's paintings to this traveling exhibition; a portrait of her, younger, softer, more fragile. Gunther boasted kind of sarcastically he could now say he's exhibited in every town along the banks of the Mississippi. I looked at it for ages and couldn't speak. I wondered if Gunther painted daily circa the time of this painting...if Glorie had been some sort of muse. He assured me it was only the one painting.

She stood there amongst idle chatter and tinkling glasses, smoking out of one of those long filter holders, filling our side of the main cabin with plumes of smoke. She has excellent posture, projects her voice, enunciates. It was in one of those moments of hers, of self-possessed, well-preserved elegance that she announced (through a heavy waft of smoke) that watching Gunther lick the seal of a joint was the most erotic experience she'd had for quite some time.

Glorie also said Gunther draws attention by shunning it; everyone has a great paradox, and that is his. His distance from the rest of the world makes him magnetic. She's right. He's just far enough away for me to feel the pull toward him. My eyes just follow him around, and the sight of him going about his measured, dreamy rituals fills me with calm.

There on the bed where he's sitting, rolling, licking, smoking, passing it to me. That's a spot on the world that's not spinning, a pocket of perfect stillness. The smaller the room, the better. The closer the walls, the tighter they hug me, the safer I feel. It's only claustrophobic if you don't want to be there. I always want to be here.

Maybe I'm being pretentious, but if I am, it's all this damn poetry he's got me reading. Novels, biographies, novellas. Novellas. Not so long ago I would have been punched for even knowing that word. Girl or no girl. My mom always maintained I was 'a bookish child', but most of those were horsey books.

He's wondering where to drop me. And he can't find a place. The world is too ugly, too plain. Every town is an empty blank. And the cities, well, they're full. As long as Gunther's acting like some weird detached dad, I'm his little girl. He says it's a sad state of affairs when the apparent predator is the protector. I don't understand what he gets all heavy about. We like it here with each other. I don't want the world to close in, but if they do, surely they'll see the innocence. Who said, 'All's fair in love and war'? I hope that applies here. I don't want him to give me up.

Once I dreamed he was a dragon, flying over all the strip malls with me dangling from his talons by the back of my shirt. He was swooping down over all that bleakness; the parking lots, the fatties waddling to their cars with mouths full of burgers, spitting crumbs…the litter, the rust, the neon, looking for a place to set me down.

And when I say something clever…Gunther likes it when I get a little insolent. He fixes those blinding eyes on me. They're like headlights. Standing there in those beaming spotlights, that starts a little jump in my chest.

We shack up in another generic hotel room. He rolls another slew of elegant joints. I type some stuff on the old typewriter. Actually, it's not old enough to be cool. It's not retro or anything, just used. It's all plastic and tacky. But it was cool of Gunther to buy it for us, although he hasn't done a damn thing on it yet. He's kind of mysterious a lot of the time. He gets up and makes a little cot look slept in, ruffled up. He does that a lot. Sometimes he even puts crumbs and wrappers on the bedclothes. But I always sleep beside him. Not with him, just next to him. I once half woke up and he had his hand on my shoulder. Like a long, still pat on the back. All full of peace, like everything else Gunther does. Usually he just sleeps on his back. I try and make it a point to wake up earlier than him. It's not easy. But I like staring at him, at his profile, in the mornings. He looks so pale. This is when I pretend he's in his coffin, and wonder again when he's going to bite me, so I can start my life with him proper.

I get up and look in the mirror. Maybe it happened in the night. No punctures; none where I can see them. And I'm so young and tan and healthy. It's all taking so damned long. The days that just drag into other days, of people glancing over and looking away, not knowing that we're special.

We go on through some more tired little towns, along some more long stretches of road dotted with take-away fast food signs. We stop in some crappy towns for some crappy food. It's not often we eat something above average. But usually it involves pie. You definitely don't want to pick anything too adventuresome on the menu. Anything European-sounding, forget it. It's just going to be a perplexing, oddly constructed, stomach-turning mess. (Gunther's words; he once got a little excited and ordered something 'cord en bleu'.) He said he thought he'd found a droplet of culture out there in the barren wasteland. Thought maybe this noisy, greasy kitchen held a captive genius. But, alas. (As if anyone still says 'alas' these days.) He said he should have known not to look for excellence, or even edibility, in a meal that shares a menu with onion rings.

I'm thinking, it was a truck stop after all. Sometimes Gunther is as stupid as the rest of us. It does all get a bit samey out here on the road, though. I don't blame him for getting his hopes up. When we get to the coast, supposedly everything's going to be cooler. The people, the places, the food. He says I'll like it there; he likes it there; he knows it well, and can leave me with a clear conscience. I don't think so; I think he'll be too used to me by then.

It's sort of a light gray day, and we pull into a drugstore parking lot. There are some kids hanging out in the lot. They're about my age, and we eye each other off. They're all black-velvety and dark. The girl is pretty pudgy. I just look straight ahead and walk past. I can feel myself almost strutting. Can they see how tons much cooler than them I am, how much more sophisticated? I have Gunther trailing behind me, gliding fluidly, like a well-trained creature of the night. I buy shampoo, some dark-blood lipstick, and some white face powder. I apply the latter two items immediately upon returning to the car. Gunther returns with some toiletries, and the same kind of typing paper he always buys (grade-A recycled), fixes those amused beams on me and says he wonders why the young try to look so old.

That was a kind of weird day that stands out more than a lot of others. When we stopped for lunch it was looking very much like it was going to be just another boring lunch in a boring town, with people giving us shifty glances, but basically ignoring us. But the waitress was really paying attention to us, to me in particular. She had blonde, sort of Marilyn Monroe-ish hair that looked like a wig. She looked about Marilyn's age, too, if Marilyn were still alive, and had stacked on a few pounds and crammed them into that uniform. She seemed nice, though. She was super friendly to me, fussing over me a lot. When I asked directions to the ladies' room she said she'd take me. She led me behind the counter, which I thought was a little unusual. Then I found myself standing in the kitchen. There was a big chef with a greasy apron pulled tautly over an enormous gut, standing in front of the stove, sharpening a huge knife. A cooking machete. He looked a little surprised to see me back there, but not enough to actually stop what he was doing. He just kept staring and sharpening. I remember thinking, 'This isn't the ladies' room.'

This old Marilyn-ie waitress took me by the shoulders. It was a little abrupt but her grip on me was steady and comforting. I didn't think she meant any harm.

She said, 'Honey, I can get you out of here.'

I said, 'What?'

She got more urgent. 'Honey, what's your name? Can you tell me your name?'

I was getting confused now and just stared.

She shouted, 'I'm Peggy! What's your name!?'

'I'm OK,' I said.

The chef sniffed, 'Ain't no kind of name,' and chuckled at his own joke.

Peggy kept on. 'What? Honey, I can get you away from him.'

I must have looked horrified, because she stopped in her tracks, quieted down a bit, and said, 'He's not your…father…is he?'

'Um,' was my best effort.

'Well, what's he—'

I'm not a good liar, and started stammering 'He's my…uncle, we're driving, my mother's dead (at which point I started crying. I don't know whether I was starting to believe my own story, or just crack under the pressure). We're driving across, I'm going to live with my grandfather.'

'Oh, honey, I'm so sorry.' And she was clutching me to that huge, ample breast, in a long, squishy waitress hug.

I can't believe she bought that panicky garble. My pants may as well have been on fire. We were pretty nervous after that. I hightailed it out front without going to the bathroom, and when I got there Gunther wasn't in our booth. He left a nice wad of bills on the table and was waiting in the car, idling, facing the exit. I got in and he drove out calmly and deliberately. We changed our route and drove out of state lines. Every time we saw a cop car we got edgy. Gunther even had me slouch down. And then he yelled, 'My God, I haven't done anything wrong!'

12

It's not often he yells. Then he muttered, 'Who am I kidding?'

That kind of broke up our routine. Things weren't as monotonous after that. There was this new excitement. Less of the old calm. We were drawing more stuff toward us. This time when we stopped at the hotel, it wasn't a two-tiered budget inn with a bored receptionist and nothing doing. It was a proper roadhouse. This town had somehow grown its own energy, or sucked it from somewhere, out past all the farms and fields. It was kind of messy, with loaded guys ambling across the parking lot with beers in their hands, shouting to people inside. I couldn't tell if they were mad or not. Gunther headed straight for the bar and ordered a drink. He sat himself down on a little stool and told me to go to the room. I must've kept standing there, because he got a little upset. Said I was too young to be drinking. I stood planted a little longer. I was just confused. Watching him roll joints half the night was part of my evening routine.

I did go back to the room; I tried to anyway. I put my stuff down on the bed and flipped through the TV channels. But I got bored. I went out to the soda machine by the parking lot and considered what flavor I might like. I could a feel a presence near me, but then, there were a lot of people floating around at this joint. I decided on orange. And in the racket of the can clunking down the chute, someone said, 'Hey.'

Now this boy was good looking. He had shoulder length, tousled, farm-boy hair. He looked slightly older than me, just enough to be interesting. I said 'hey' back. We talked a little and before I knew it, we were around the corner kissing. I hadn't done much kissing. I'd spent all my previous kisses wondering what the heck those guys thought they were doing, and whether or not I liked it.

I liked this kissing. And the touching. He was holding me tighter and tighter, and he was warm. His shirt was scratchy, and I don't usually know what texture people's clothes are. All the closeness was kind of nice. I was liking the kissing more and more as it went on. Then we stopped for kind of a breather. We just chatted. Small talk and stuff. He asked where I was from. I said back East. I found his presence kind of exciting, but his talking was boring me. Gunther hates small talk. 'Abhors' it. Says it's a needless strain on the vocal cords. He usually gets by with a polite grunt, and I think I agree with him, that's usually 'sufficient'. People aren't really interested in you anyway. I hoped this boy would get back to the kissing. I've got Gunther to talk to if talking's what I want.

I guess I was boring him, too, because he got back to the kissing, and pretty quickly too. I don't know how long we kept at it. He had started to touch other parts of me. At first I was uncomfortable with some of it, like when he swept his big old country-boy paw across my breasts. But then I started to get kind of tingly. And then Gunther shouted, 'What the HELL do you think you're doing?!' It was clear he'd been back to the room, because he'd taken his jacket off. I wondered how long he'd been looking for me. I had no idea how long I'd been out there. Long enough to get pretty tingly. It was all kind of a blur from there. Gunther marched me straight back to the room, barely glanced at the boy, who muttered, 'Jeez, your dad is pretty uptight.'

Once back in the room we didn't really say much. Gunther rolled an assembly line of joints with a series of jerky movements that had none of his usual joint-rolling grace or finesse. He was glaring at his hands, glaring at everything they touched. I mumbled 'sorry', and he snorted. I didn't think I'd done anything hugely wrong, but it was late, I guess. He must have been looking for me for a while. But as far as I knew we were both entertaining ourselves. That was his idea. I thought he was having a night on the town. Or on the roadhouse, as it were. And me…well, as Glorie announced huskily when I stood staring at her traveling portrait, you're only young once.

He seemed back to normal by the next morning, when he was doing all his morning things. By the time we got into the car he was a lot sunnier, for him. He seemed to have seen something funny in it. He smiled; not his usual beaming, but he glanced a weakish grin my direction. 'So our little girl is growing up,' he said. 'I think you can do better than Random Farm Boy.' We drove a ways further, past another doughnut sign, with faded, chipping paint. 'Perhaps, a little more discerning.'

We didn't deviate from routine for a couple of weeks at least, after that incident. We each seemed to be making a concerted effort to keep things as regular as possible. We didn't even make fun of people, or towns, or signs. We didn't complain about the boringness of anything. We preserved it. We damn near cultivated it.

I just wanted to crawl back into that bubble of safeness, that cocoon of hugging walls, smoke, and gazing at Gunther; basking in his benevolence, and dreaming of the promise of ultimate freedom he might deliver. For his part, I think he was trying to regain his composure, his suave air. I think he was largely succeeding.

We were on sort of an artificial roll. I say 'artificial' because we weren't quite ourselves. We were both a little nervy. But that didn't seem to hurt us. The fact that we weren't so locked into our comfy groove together meant we were able to put more of our individual vibes out into the world. We managed to charm our way through several towns. People were actually starting to think I was his nice little daughter. We weren't creeping people out anymore.

Maybe we've been getting too charismatic for our own good. Because we decided to hit the town again last night, and this time together. People thought it was cute I was hanging around. But then Gunther started talking to a pretty lady at the bar. I'd been sitting at the booth for a while, and it didn't look like he was ordering us any food. In fact, it looked like he was buying them both a drink. And she was laughing.

I never have much money of my own, so when I need to buy my own meals I usually head for a vending machine. Vending machines must be romantic beacons for me, because when I got to this one there was a nice-looking boy there; kind of punky with dyed black hair, and sort of a shy slouch. He was buying an oversized chocolate chip cookie. We said 'hey'. He said that was his dinner. I got a candy bar and said, 'Mine, too.'

The candy bar was gross. He said I should have gotten a cookie; his was good. And filling. I said I didn't have enough change. So he talked me into letting him buy me one, and we went outside and sat on the curb by the parking lot. His talking was more interesting than the farm boy's. I didn't know what he was on about half the time, but at least he sounded like *he* knew, sounded smart. He was talking about music and anti-mainstream stances. He didn't ask me any dumb small-talky questions. He mostly just talked about himself.

By now I thought it was time we got to the

kissing. He was a boy, and I was pretty sure that's what boys want. I leaned in, but he didn't seem to get the point. In fact, he kind of melted into an even more closed posture. He was almost folding in on himself. We talked some more, and then he got onto the subject of how girls like me never like guys like him. I asked him what a girl like me was, and he didn't elaborate. He just stayed all slouchy. I definitely had to kiss him now. To make him feel better, and to show him he was wrong. So I did, and he seemed kind of startled, but then warmed into the kissing nicely. He wasn't as pushy as the farm boy. He was softer. This was nice. I got all tingly faster. We stayed out there in the parking lot like that for a while, swapping spit and lightly pawing each other. He said a few nice things to me, about me being pretty and all that. Then he said we should go back to his room. Apparently his parents had got him his own room, with a balcony and everything. I thought that seemed like a bad idea, and I knew Gunther would be upset. In fact, that suggestion brought me crashing back to earth. I said I better go, and went back to our room.

Gunther wasn't there. He came in just after dawn, looking disheveled and weary. He avoided looking me in the eye and flopped onto his bed, fetal position. Clothes and all. This room had twin beds, instead of two double, or one double and one cot. He stayed like that until he got up to take a shower. He went through his morning routine, and eventually looked very refreshed. He was calmer than he has been of late on today's drive, and even more polite than usual.

He returned and kept to his civilized ways and his reclusive rituals for a while after that night. He was reading good books and talking about ideas and ideals with me, just like old times, smoking away. I was typing loads on the tacky typewriter, smoking with him. We had some interesting discussions, and sometimes when we were stoned I could make him laugh a lot, then he would beam. And, as I'm sure I've mentioned, I like it when he shines those eyes on me. I felt comfortable again, but I wouldn't say I felt the old safety.

The next few days' driving was affable and chatty. One thing I probably haven't stressed about Gunther is that he is very down to earth. For all his cultured-ness, he likes talking my crap with me. He likes hearing my silly stories. He's got a few of his own. He's quick with a laugh, or rather, quick with a sharp-toothed grin.

We didn't collect as many suspicious looks when we stopped for meals, as we passed through this latest assortment of localities. We were comfortable. Maybe it was also the fact we weren't in the middle of the country anymore. It's less scary-weird when you get closer to the edges. People are just more normal. You don't feel followed by countless pairs of accusing eyes, hovering just out of sight. Walking down Main Street in Averageville Anywhere, Middle-of-the-Country is like walking through a clearing, feeling that all around you, the trees, bushes, hell…sky, are full of things itching to pounce.

Gunther says that is the folly of a country so large, and so insular. It becomes its own planet. The parts that aren't visited enough by outside influences repel those influences when they come across them. So they just get more and more stuck in their own strange way of being. I'm from a small town myself, but, being closer to one of the edges, I guess it was a little more idyllic.

We were coming into the desert now, and the landscape was interesting to look at. There were still a lot of farms dotted about, so it wasn't moonscape desert. We'd get into that later. It was good to have a change of scenery. All those strip malls and scrubby trees were starting to hurt my eyes. I'd spent half my time just watching Gunther drive: staring out ahead serenely, hypnotizing the road with those cool beams.

I spent less time typing during the evenings that accompanied these days, and more time studying Gunther. He was so used to me now he didn't seem to notice, or mind. But then he never seemed to mind anything. That was probably why I felt so safe with him, and why all that safety came like a rush when we first started spending all this time together. There were no sudden moves, no shifts or jolts, he was just smooth, just there. It was like being under water. I've made him mad by now a few times, obviously. That burst my bubble a little, but it also made him more human. We had a comfortable closeness now, definitely. But he still kept a dignified distance. Just far enough for me to contemplate him. I know we like each other's companionship. I sometimes thought it was kind of pointless, having random make-out sessions in nowhere towns with boys I didn't even know. There was an arbitrariness and lack of taste to these encounters. It seemed dumb to pick them over someone classy like Gunther. I couldn't tell if it bothered him. He was pretty cool and contained, and had his own occasional encounters, so it was hard to tell. By now I had gotten a taste for the kissing, and was starting to wonder what it would be like to kiss him.

We seem to be zig-zagging across the country. We certainly aren't moving in a straight line. Gunther has a few friends scattered around the place. Quite a few really, for a reclusive sort. We've been stopping here and there to visit these various characters. You'd have to be a little out there to know Gunther. And then we stopped in other places and I didn't know why. I get the impression it has been a while since he's visited these people, these spots, and that's part of why he is going out of his way. Getting to the far coast where the living is better is simply a bonus now, a minor detail. At this point I'm along for the ride.

After several days of lazy driving and laid-back stopovers, we've kicked back into gear. Gunther high-tailed it all day to get to this town where his friend Murray lives. When we got there it was well past dark, and his eyes were squinty and strained. He looked tired, and I thought not very excited to see an old friend. Some things are more of an obligation, though. When we got there Murray was sitting on the front porch in a rocking chair. It was all woodsy and dark. There was a warm orange glow filling the inside of the cottage, lighting up all the rustic clutter. He got up and gave us both a warm welcome. Gunther handed him a package wrapped loosely in cloth, or leather or something. Murray laughed heartily, then nodded, put it in the pocket of his big suede coat, and led us inside. That old shack was such a stereotype I thought it looked like a movie set. It amused me someone actually lived like that, full-time, all year round. This wasn't some fishing trip. He actually had a real moose head on his wall. And rifles. There was a roaring log fire, tartan blankets scattered everywhere, and of course, a bear skin rug that I thought looked like road kill. I don't really like dead things.

We sat around the big log table for ages. Murray served up a fairly substantial meal, which consisted of meat, meat, and more meat, with some bloody gravy, and a mash on the side that may have once been a vegetable. Those two were drinking red wine. I was on cherry soda. Gunther can hold his alcohol, but Murray was starting to talk a whole lot of shit that I didn't care to hear. Stuff about Gunther's playboy past; what a stud he used to be, how many delicate hearts he shattered as he fucked his way through a smorgasbord of hot babes of all description. And in perfect accompaniment to these orgies were all the drugs. Was there anything he hadn't tried, any path he hadn't merrily sauntered down? I stole a glance at Gunther. I didn't like to hear his dignity affronted like this. He looked weary, but unfazed. At length he said, 'Yes, I suppose I was a bit of a hedonist back then.' Murray raised his glass as far as his fat arm could stretch above his fat stomach and exclaimed, 'What a life, what a fucking life!'

Murray didn't look so good this morning. Last night, lit by firelight, various lamps, and the rosy glow of red wine in his cheeks, he was heartily robust. Standing in the hallway outside the bathroom door, in a white(ish) wifebeater with a towel over his shoulder, he looked like a surprised albino walrus. Doughy and pallid, with whiskers puffing out everywhere and tiny pink bloodshot eyes.

'Hello, sunshine,' he said.

I said 'hi'.

He made Gunther and me pancakes, and he made a hell of a lot of them. It was quite a production. It was nice to be in a house again, even if it was a house full of weirdo dead trophies and innuendo. It was still cozy. And all that crap about home-cooked meals being incomparable is true. Gunther said something to that effect, and I was just thinking the same thing. You can't go wrong with a six-inch stack of pancakes.

Still, it was good to get back on the road. It's become sort of a home in itself. I asked Gunther if he had really done all that stuff Murray said he had back there. Gunther said basically, yeah, although it wasn't quite as heartless, or soulless, or lamely macho as Murray made it all sound. He said back then if he wanted to try something, he tried it. He satiated his appetites and curiosity, but not at the expense of others. Like attracts like, he said. Suddenly I didn't feel so bad about it all, didn't feel like Gunther was in any danger of falling from grace. It was devil-may-care. Fearless. Almost gallant.

He said, 'I just had too much energy.'

I said, 'But it's probably made you a lot calmer now.'

'Yeah,' he gave a little snort. 'Or maybe just tired.'

Our next stop was a terribly bright diner perched on a hill, in kind of a cute, bland, medium-sized town. It looked like a plastic gingerbread house, although I don't think that was intentional. The waitress not only added to the effect, she brought it right over the top. She had on a hot pink, body-hugging minidress uniform. The name Taffy was sewn on a badge that teetered on the precipice of one of her ginormous tits. I suspect she had on one of those pointy 1950s-style bras. Those two blinding hot pink horizontal peaks were just jutting out like no one's business. It's like they were trying to make some kind of statement, irrespective of the rest of her.

I ordered pancakes again, which amused us both, but that's all I was in the mood for. Taffy leaned over Gunther every time either of them spoke, straight-backed, chest out, topless-dancer style. She had long yellow blonde hair, which she dangled over him. I think it tickled his face. She looked like she belonged in a heavy metal video. Gunther said he was waiting for the band to pop out, and wondered if we were going to have to start lip-syncing. It was all kind of hilarious, but damned if it didn't make me a little jealous. She had on the highest heels of any waitress I've ever seen. I thought all waitresses wore flat shoes. But I didn't see many customers so I figured she must go out the back and put her feet up a lot. Then again, some women can wear heels all the time; they really are that glamorous.

After that we were in for another long stint of serious driving. Gunther's brow was really furrowed for this one. We were headed for this lady's house, Stephanie. Gunther said her husband died a few months back. He didn't say how. He was a fine man, he said, and there would be a lot of sadness in this house.

She lives in a bigger town than most we've visited so far, more of a smallish city. It's not very lively, though. Kind of industrial and basic. Stephanie lives in the suburbs, in a two-storey house with a cute front porch and a small yard that spills into the neighbor's.

When we pulled up she was standing on the porch, wearing a billowy sun dress. She had long brown hair that fell straight down in subtle waves, with a fringe just over her eyes. I thought she cut an attractive figure up there. She was managing a little smile.

We got out of the car and headed straight for her, didn't start unloading or anything. She gave me a dazed glance, and kind of fell into Gunther's arms, all floppy like. She just stayed there for a while until Gunther began to extract himself.

'You look well,' he said.

She didn't say 'Thanks' or 'So do you', or anything polite like that. She just gave him a tired, exasperated look that took her a while to make.

Gunther introduced us girls, and she showed me to my room; a puny box at the end of a hallway decked out in D.I.Y. picture frames and random crocheted thingies. I got the feeling she wanted me to stay there. Maybe she just assumed, me being a teenager and all, that I would want to hole up in my room. Naturally that was not the case, and I went downstairs again to check out the house and hear what those two were talking about. She'd be fixing us a snack soon, I figured.

When I got down there, Gunther was making three cups of tea. Stephanie took three sugars. That was a lot for a skinny lady, I thought. I thought a lady like that would be all princessy about watching her figure. I took her tea in, and Gunther came in behind with ours. I perched myself on the far end of Stephanie's couch. Gunther sat across from her in an armchair.

He said, 'So please, Stephanie, tell me how you have been.'

There was a long pause, during which I thought she shot me a grumpy look.

'Oh, all right considering, I guess,' she said at length. 'I'm hangin' in there.' Then she looked at me and snapped, 'Would you like to watch some TV?'

I said, 'No thanks, that's OK.'

And Gunther said I was perfectly capable of carrying on an adult discussion, and grasping her unfortunate situation. Which was nice of him, I thought, because I hadn't given him much of an indication that I cared one way or the other.

She said it was hard with Ward gone. He hadn't prepared, so there was the financial hardship. She missed the companionship. Apparently they had been having their problems, and she felt it was a bad note to leave things on, for all eternity. I pictured a bad note, resonating. Eternally. That must be an uncomfortable feeling. I wondered if she meant to be that poetic, but it didn't seem so, it seemed like her words were just tumbling out.

Gunther was sitting back in his chair with one leg crossed over the other, listening with his usual air of attentive stillness. It must be nice for her to talk to Gunther, I thought. It must be nice to be sitting there in all his attention.

She still hadn't offered us any snacks. And then she started drinking. Gunther declined, which isn't like him. He always accepts the hospitality of his friends. He likes his 'social rituals'. Maybe that's a leftover from his hedonistic days. I know what he's on about, though. I was a cigarette smoker for a little while. Me and my friend Heather started smoking the day she turned eighteen. It was always more fun smoking with someone else; offering the pack, lighting their cigarettes, getting them to light mine…

Gunther rose and stood over Stephanie, who was clutching a glass of straight Southern Comfort with both hands. He asked if he could make us anything to eat; would she like anything, was there perhaps a restaurant nearby. Pizza place?

'I'm not hungry!' she spat. 'I'm sorry, I'm a shitty hostess.'

'Stephanie, you've been through a lot.' Ever calm. 'Let me get you something to eat.'

He ran through a few options, but got no response from her. I said I could go a pizza, so we found her phone book and ordered a large margherita with mushrooms, delivered.

Now that bitch ate nearly the whole pizza. And I know I should be nicer, with her a grieving widow and all, but she said she wasn't hungry. And she was being damned ungrateful to Gunther, and he's a decent friend to have. I don't know where she put it all. She still looked perfect in her fancy flowery sundress (just a bit hunched over).

Someone started banging on the screen door, shouting, 'Hey! Stephie, you in there? I thought I smelled pizza!' followed by some snorts of goofy laughter.

The keeper of that voice was something to behold. He was one of those self-made rednecks. As in, he looked like hell, but it seemed like that was a look he'd cultivated.

There was the greasy black hair, slicked back and up in a partially collapsing bouffant. Probably what Elvis' hair looked like the day he died. Then there was the tracksuit top, unzipped past his navel, to expose a yellowing undershirt, and some formidable tufts of chest hair. A chest toupee. And, yeah, he had a medallion dangling over that gorilla plumage. He was barefoot, with tight faded Levis cinched under his gut by a Playboy belt buckle. I thought that finished the look nicely; I'd never seen someone that white trash so close up. And that is really saying something. Because, like I said, I come from a small town, and Gunther and I have been everywhere now.

'Just kidding you all,' he boomed, 'I saw the pizza truck pull up.'

Stephanie perked up a little, and said self-consciously, 'This is Jimmy, my um…' she gave a weak but perky smile, 'neighbor.'

Gunther said, 'Pleasure to meet you.' I almost laughed out loud. It cracks me up how overly polite he is to people I know he finds the most uncouth.

'Well la dee da indeed,' was the witty rejoinder. 'Where are you folks from?' His attention immediately shifted to the empty pizza box. 'None left?'

'No, sorry. I would have invited you over, but…' Stephanie seemed to have bitten off more than she could chew with this obnoxious white trash prick. He sat down and put his hand on her knee in a manner that could only be called proprietary. A shadow crossed Gunther's face.

Eventually Jimmy got tired of rambling on to us. We weren't offering much up in the way of replies, and I guess he got hungry. He probably knew now the pizza was gone, Stephanie's house didn't promise much in the way of food. He got up and left as abruptly as he'd entered.

I should have been quicker to grab those slices. But I like to watch my etiquette around Gunther. Eventually the hunger pangs got the better of me. That, and I was bored of listening to Stephanie dribble on to Gunther, tired of her shooting me sulky looks. So I got up and did a cardinal no-no. I didn't see what difference it made if I was a bad house-guest; she was such a damn shocking host. I slipped into her kitchen and started rifling through her cupboards, fridge, drawers. I was thinking chocolate chip cookies would do nicely, but I wasn't feeling overly choosy. Just anything remotely tasty would do.

This is where I started to feel properly sorry for her. I didn't see *anything* remotely tasty. She had things like plain crackers, and celery stalks. Cottage cheese, vanilla diet shakes, vitamin pills, raisins, whole wheat bread gone mouldy, low-fat milk. Here she was, trying to keep herself attractive, it seemed. A fat lot of good it had done her.

I poured myself a Diet RC Cola on the rocks and headed back in.

Stephanie was on her feet, teasingly swaying in Gunther's general direction, in a sultry swaggery dance. And then her arms were around his neck.

He said, 'Stephanie...' and nodded at me, standing in the doorway.

She said, 'What *is* it with the kid?'

Gunther said nothing.

'Seriously, it's a little weird, don't you think?'

I was waiting for him to say something witty like, 'Personally, I think you and Jimmy is a little weird.' But he didn't. He just sat there, absorbing.

She had another go at kissing him. He fended her off. He laid his hands on her shoulders and gently pushed her back down to her seat on the couch. Only Gunther could make shoving off someone's unwanted advances look like an act of delicate kindness. Suddenly he was on the couch with her, wrapping his arms around her, saying, 'Sorry, so sorry.'

I imagine he meant sorry her dead husband was dead. That's why people usually say 'sorry' to someone who's just lost a loved one. Maybe he meant sorry to see her in such a state, behaving like a total scrag and consorting with Jimmy. Or maybe he meant sorry he couldn't kiss her because he was in fact secretly in love with me. I considered whether she would make a good Soulmate of Eternal Darkness for

Gunther, and decided that would be a lot of whining to put up with until the end of time. Besides, I bet I'm a quicker learner. She sat on the edge of the couch, looking wide-eyed and subdued. She really did look pretty then, even with a dripping ring of migrating make-up pooling under each eye.

Eventually Gunther hauled her off to bed. Tucked her in, I imagine. Then he and I sat outside on the porch and smoked a joint. He wasn't himself. I stopped feeling like I was there, so I went inside to bed. I don't know what time he came in.

The next morning I got up and took a shower, fussed around for a while in my room. I didn't hear anyone else about, so I figured everyone must still be asleep. Gunther was taking the couch, even though he was much too tall for it. I ventured into the living room eventually, and he was nowhere to be seen. I looked around and then thought, 'Jeez, he didn't give in and bone Stephanie, did he?' I sat around in a bored, unimpressed vigil, waiting for those two to sheepishly rear their heads.

After a while I heard Stephanie let out a moan upstairs. I wandered outside onto the porch, lest I be subjected to more of these moans. I was glaring into space, letting my eyes bore into the empty driveway, when it hit me. The car was gone! Fucking gone! No car, no…Where the fuck was Gunther?

It struck me all at once how joined at the hip we've become, what a unit. He doesn't just go someplace and not tell me where: he is never out of my sight. I tried to calm myself down. He's Mr. Considerate, I thought. There's no (edible) food in the house, and us ladies were both asleep; he's probably gone out to get us all some breakfast. And then my mind was full again, with warm meditations on Gunther's benevolence, and the possibility of a generously portioned meal.

I sat on the porch and waited awhile. I remember thinking, 'Man, the service must be slow in this town.' Then I went inside and watched TV. Stephanie came downstairs and said, 'Where's Gunther?' and I said I didn't know, probably getting breakfast. She said it was past noon. She had a note pinned to her chest. That was unmistakably Gunther's angular cursive. How hilarious, I thought, he must think this chick is a serious idiot. That's one step removed from taping the note to her forehead.

It read:

You are right. It is of questionable judgment for an old thing like me to keep the company of so young a girl, (although I have done no deliberate wrong). Perhaps you can keep her with you until suitable accommodation can be found.

He then added, in a different color ink: *Perhaps a passage to San Francisco could be arranged for her.*

I was pointing at the note, simultaneously alerting Stephanie to its presence, and reading it. I could feel my mouth dropping open. Being abandoned by Gunther...being without Gunther, that was a horrible prospect. But being stuck here with Stephanie, that was a close second.

'What the...Wow.' Stephanie was a lot softer when she wasn't drinking or crying. Or both. From what I have seen, the two go hand in hand.

After a minute she said, 'Well...I guess we better get some breakfast.'

We rode bikes. She rode her late husband Ward's, and I rode hers. It was downright wholesome. I hadn't seen she didn't have a car. I thought, 'Sheesh, the old man didn't leave her a pot to poo in.' And she was an artist. Well, more of a craftsperson, really. She had homemade stuff hanging up all over the place. No wonder she was crying all the time.

But it turns out she wasn't crying all the time. Last night must have been a rough night. I chuckled to myself that seeing Gunther would stir any woman up. And then I promptly fell to sulking over his cruel departure.

We went to a neighborhood café that had a lot more character than I would have expected, judging from its surroundings for miles around. It was cozy. I ordered pancakes. Stephanie got scrambled eggs, and gobbled them up, pizza-style. I thought, someone with an appetite like hers should keep more food around the house. And then I wondered whether she is always so hungry because she never does have any damn food. It makes no sense for her to deprive herself like that.

When I asked her why her house was so empty she said, 'Because no one lives there.'

That really bummed me out. And it kind of didn't make sense. It was one of those vague melancholy statements old people make, that are meant to sound deep. How old do you have to be before you start saying things like that? I sure as hell don't talk that way.

She asked me a lot of questions about Gunther; me and Gunther, that is. I wasn't giving much away. I've never had a friend like Gunther before. I don't know what's allowed. I haven't had many good friends, full stop. And when I do find one, I'm never choosy about the circumstances. I think that's pretty ungrateful, to be all picky. When I was nine, I had a friend who was only five. I know that's young, but I thought she was damn smart for her age. And when my family spent summers up in Maine, I used to hang out with an old fisherman. He would fix me up with a fishing line and I'd sit there next to him on the sunny docks, listening to him philosophize, old-man style, hour after hour. I didn't actually like catching fish. It was thrilling and satisfying, after all that sitting, but violent, too. It shattered the calm. And I went through a phase where I used to jerk the line sideways every time and inadvertently hook them in the eye. Les had to take them off the hook for me. If they were big enough, he cleaned and gutted them too.

I've never had many friends my own age. They switch around between friends a lot, and I never know when we're friends and when we aren't. I just don't understand all that, and end up drifting off and forgetting about them. I guess I'm the all or nothing type. I'm either all alone, or never alone. Because when I have someone close, I like to draw them in properly close, and bask in their company a lot. I don't know when the next lonely expanse of friendlessness will be. I like to think never. I think that every time.

So there was Stephanie, picking apart Gunther and me. And friendship is a sacred thing. There was a note of sympathy in her voice that was comforting, but unnerving. She was giving the impression she cared about me, which made me open up a little. But then, she was acting like our friendship, mine and Gunther's, was something she should feel sorry for me about. She'd made it pretty crystal clear she'd like to get a lot closer to him herself. You don't see me standing over him grinding my pelvis into the back of his armchair. I just leave him be.

So there's nothing wrong with her throwing her drunken self at him, but there is with me and him being roadtripping adventurers together. Man, I really didn't feel like accepting her pity on that point. And I was getting increasingly shitty on the whole subject. All this talk about me and Gunther seemed moot, now that he had just fucking left me there. My shock was giving way to a rising panic.

We rode back to her place, and she pottered around, tidying up for a while. Her place already was fairly tidy, but in a weird way. She had things scooped up into stacks, every few feet; magazines, balls of yarn, newspapers, books...All these little piles of stuff were orderly, but it did look like they might avalanche if anyone touched them. So she was going through them and staring at things, then dividing them into more piles. I assumed a lot of these new ones must have been trash piles. She even had an old Playboy. She didn't try to hide it from me. I figured she could tell I'm not that shockable. But it was more likely she was just zoning out, not even noticing me. Let's face it; this lady really does have a foot in the grave.

Then she sat down on the couch and started trying to nut out what to do with me. It was pretty clear she had no idea, but pawning me off seemed to be her first inclination. She had toyed with a 'two girls on the town' theme over breakfast, but that seemed to have worn off. Now she was asking about my family, and even mentioned foster care—two words that will make any teenager break into a cold sweat. Which I did.

I cursed Gunther anew for leaving, for breaking the unspoken bond of Road Buddies. You don't just deposit someone somewhere, midway through a mission. I felt like the heavens should open; felt an act so unholy should at least warrant some kind of mini apocalypse. The sun beating down on all those quaint, well-kept lawns, the birds chirping, the dude washing his car, sending classic rock gently wafting over the block…This was all making me edgy. This environment is indifferent to my pain, indifferent to any pain at all.

I went for a walk and got us some doughnuts. And bagels. And a few other things I thought seemed enticing. (Gunther had left us some cash. Jerk.) I was hoping to spark some kind of feeding frenzy in the ever-ravenous Stephanie. My aim was to stall her; get her to chill the fuck out. At least then I could sort out a plan, instead of her trying to plan everything for me. Plus when someone is that flighty, it's only natural to try to get them to relax. They're bad company, otherwise. I couldn't leave straight away for various reasons. The most pressing of these was the belief that Gunther would turn around and come back for me. He needed to know where to find me, so I had to stay put.

It sort of worked. She was touched to see all that food. And we did have a big therapeutic pig-out (her words). Then we cleared most of it away and made some space on the table. We were going to make some of her artsy-craftsy stuff together. I had been asking her about it all. My father once told me women like it when you ask them to talk about themselves. I think he said it mainly to demonstrate his pulling power with the opposite sex. Tips on how to seduce women don't come in that handy if you already happen to be one. However, this one did because there she was, chattering away, showing me how to glue this and bend that, and finally calming the hell down.

I needed money. That was for damned sure. When we were done making all that frilly stuff and hanging it up around the house, she sent me out for milk, which was perfect. It gave me a chance to trawl for jobs. I went into every place between Steph's and the convenience mart, asking if they had any work going. I even asked at the shoe repair hut.

I ended up passing the convenience store and heading into downtown proper. I was feeling determined. Though after the sun went down there was almost no one around. People shouted in the distance. Cars drove past, and an empty bus.

I came across a lady, taking up the whole sidewalk in front of me, the way some people just have a lot of presence. She was damn pretty, and seemed to know it. She had on knee-high boots and a plain black dress. Her hair was all clean and flowy. It was clear she was somehow affiliated with the dark and nondescript building she was loitering in front of. The way she was strutting around the place was plain intimidating, but I'd made up my mind to ask everywhere. She was already starting to smirk at me, but when I opened my mouth to ask about jobs, *that* got her laughing good and proper. I had to stand there and wait until she'd stopped. I didn't know whether to be insulted because I was being laughed at, or what. When she stopped, she looked me square in the face, pretty seriously. She must have still thought I was a bit of an idiot, but was now grateful for the huge laugh I'd given her.

She said blandly, 'See what gives.'

She went inside, and finally resurfaced when I was thinking of wandering off dejectedly. She had a girl with her.

She said, 'This is no place for little girls. Maybe Loren here can sort you out.'

Loren wasn't much older than me, if at all. But she was all done up fancy, and so had an air of maturity. She also had a tiny plasticky dress, orangey-blonde hair pulled up in a high pony tail, bright pink lipstick that matched her dress, and every other kind of make-up you could think of. She started walking me down the block. She too looked a touch amused at my expense.

'So you wanna be a dancer.'

This statement caught me off guard, and 'Uh…' was my only reply.

'You *can* dance?' she snapped.

'Well, yeah,' I said, 'can't everyone?'

She let out a snorty laugh. 'You'd be surprised.'

We turned a corner in the direction of some thumping music. There were neon signs with silhouettes of busty women arching backwards. I should have had an inkling it was that kind of dancing. I sort of did, but was too hell-bent on getting a job to care about the particulars.

She nodded at the doorman, and we marched into the thick of it. It was everything you'd think it would be, just like any strip club I'd seen in the movies, or on TV cop shows. No more, no less. Maybe some of the girls were a little rougher around the edges, but that was kind of raw and sexy, I guess. I mean, isn't that what people come here for, to see someone up close? If Gunther were here, we'd be talking this over. But then if Gunther were here, I wouldn't be.

There were quite a few ladies in the audience. That was the only major difference I could spot between this and the fictitious strip clubs I'd seen. Hollering up a storm. They seemed to be enjoying it more than most of the guys, who were just sitting there struck dumb. Surely they'd seen a naked lady before. Christ! I wondered if the girls cared, if they got sick of all those stupid fucks staring up at them.

I asked Loren. She didn't bat an eye. 'You care how much money they cram into your g-string.'

She walked me up to a greasy fat guy and said, 'Hey, Carlo, you got any work for her?'

Like the rest of them, Carlo looked amused to see me. 'I'm looking for *it*,' he said, 'and I don't think I see it. What are you, twelve?'

'No!' I snapped.

He held a chubby hand up to my neck. 'Yeah, but from here down you're twelve.'

'Carlo!' Loren gave a shocked laugh.

'I'm seventeen.' Then I added, 'and a half!'

'If you're still talkin' in halves, you're too fuckin' young.' He had me there. We stood looking at each other for a few seconds. Then he said, 'Beat it, Babycakes.'

Loren came up behind me and put a hand on my

shoulder. She pushed me ahead of her and guided me briskly through the dazed men and screaming broads, toward the exit, in her warm officious grip. I was stewing over Carlo's parting remarks. 'Beat it Babycakes', I repeated to myself. Who talks like that? Did he get that line out of a movie? It's bad enough his club has to be a complete stereotype; he has to be one, too?

Loren gave me one last push out the door, and said, 'Oh well, you tried. See ya.'

'Yeah,' I said. 'See ya.'

By now it was dark, and this looked to be a pretty scummy part of town. But the wrong side of the tracks vibe was quickly ruined by a picture-perfect family having a Hallmark moment across the street. Both parents were leaning adoringly over a toddler in her stroller, looking ridiculously cute in a Little Red Riding Hood coat. Mom was adjusting the hood. Dad was stroking Mom's back. A little boy with blond ringlets was looking on, smiling.

I didn't want to go home jobless, but it was pointless staying out there much later. I still hadn't gotten milk, though. And damn it if there wasn't a Help Wanted sign up in the convenience store. The guy wanted to train me up then and there. He said I could finish up the evening shift. It was just him on that night. I worked a couple of hours, then headed for home with a quart of milk. He told me I could have four nights a week, 6:00 to 12:00, and some afternoon shifts.

Stephanie was mad as hell when I finally got home. The house was quiet and mostly dark. The front porch light was on. I got in and closed the door. I said hello to see if she was around. I didn't hear anything back. I put the milk in the fridge. And then the yelling started, from the back of the house. She must have been sitting in the den.

'I was gonna call the cops, you know!'

That she cared when I came and went surprised me. I just stood there.

'Where in God's name were you at for so long? At this time of night?'

'I got a job.'

'You…what? What kind of job do you get at midnight?'

'I got it at 9:30.'

'You could have at least called.'

'I don't have your number.'

'Well, you can't stay here. I can't you have flitting around all hours.'

She didn't even ask me what the job was. Man, she didn't give a crap about me. When you get in trouble with adults, it never is about you. It's about them, and how losing track of you makes them look like a bad person. Except Gunther, he didn't care enough about what other people thought until this bitch went and shot off her mouth. All because she knew she wasn't going to get laid that night, and she was all weepy and horny.

By the time I got to bed, I was in a dark mood. Where the hell was Gunther? I got a job; that was good. But I couldn't go anywhere yet, so I had to win over Stephanie all over again, when I didn't actually give a crap what she thought. And where the fuck was Gunther? Where was his breathing? How was I supposed to get to sleep? He can't be gone for good; we're so…unfinished. That note he safety-pinned to Stephanie's tits…man, I can't fathom how he thinks he's taking the high road. His absence is his greatest insult. It is more than an insult. It's everything I hate about the world; the violence, the pathos, all the crazy shit that goes down, the fear, the needless suffering that marks so many lives. It's all that, encapsulated in the blinding pain of finding myself alone in a Gunther-less world.

I sensed an enormous encroaching emptiness; could practically picture it hovering outside the walls of Stephanie's featureless guest room. Hell, if he had any class, if he was anything like what I had him cracked up to be (and this is where I let my imagination get away from me again), he'd come flying up here and tap on my window. Damn it. If people can believe in God, why can't I believe in vampires? There is no other practical explanation for teeth so pointy.

I ended up sleeping half the next day away. When I got downstairs Stephanie was slumped on the couch, knitting one of her multi-media creations. She looked up and said, 'Hey.'

I said, 'Morning.'

She grinned and said, 'Afternoon.'

I headed into the kitchen and saw a tired-looking plate of scrambled eggs sitting on the counter. Stephanie overtook me and put this in the microwave. She took some O.J. out of the fridge and plonked it on the table. There was already a glass.

She said, 'There's bread if you want toast.'

I said, 'No, thanks', and then changed my mind, and got up and made myself some toast.

'I'm brewing a pot of coffee. Do you want some?' Jeez, housewife extraordinaire.

I said, 'Yeah, OK.'

I ate in hungry silence. Then Stephanie sat down with our coffees and said, 'Look, you can stay here a while if you have to. We just need to work a few things out.'

I said, 'Yeah, OK,' again.

The next several days were spent working and sleeping, sleeping and working. The job was OK. I saw and talked to a lot of people, but it was mostly boring interactions, or transactions, as it were. I wasn't there to make friends. The boss was a predictable and generic dead-end job authority figure, boring and pushy but basically harmless. Nothing ever had any point to it. So what if this is past its sell-by date, just put it in the bargain bin. Did I remember to put out the new super crunchy chips? Did I know to put them next to the regular crunchy, not the plain? We needed to organize them according to ascending crunchiness.

Usually I was the only one on my shift, but sometimes I overlapped with one of the other workers, usually Chris. If Chris was putting stock out he used to shout things at the boss the whole time, like, 'Hey Dale, where do these measure on the crunchometer?' or 'Yo Dale, in the World of Chocolate, do peanuts go next to almonds, or are they gonna fight?'

It was nice to be earning some money. And Stephanie could tell me some stuff she needed from the store, and I could bring it home for her. Usually I told her not to pay me for it. It's not like I was paying rent. She said that was silly, and shoved money at me anyway. Sometimes I brought stuff home of my own accord, and just put it away in secret. Like ice cream. Stephanie wasn't nearly as ravenous as she was before. She ate at regular mealtimes, pretty much, and not like a starving dog. She ate normal amounts, like the rest of us. And stopped if she was full.

One night I came home pretty tired, as usual. I could hear a big argument booming out over the last few blocks of my walk to Stephanie's. I thought 'Glad that's not my house', and when I got there, it was. Jimmy was on the front porch hollering like a stuck pig. Stephanie was saying things like: 'Look it's just not a good time right now, I'm sorry.' And 'You've been…a wonderful help…I just need to be in my own space right now, I think.'

He bellowed, 'What, now that you're playing mommy?'

Steph said gently, 'She has nothing to do with it. I'm sorry Jimmy, I'm gonna ask you to go home.'

I didn't know whether to advance onto the porch or not. Needless to say, it was awkward. But he was so worked up I thought maybe he was going to do something stupid, like hit her. He was looming over her, sort of twitching. She looked bravely unmoved, just stared up at his face. That was it, I got up there and marched through the two of them. He started back in surprise, then let out a big snort, finally turned on his heels and left.

We went inside. Stephanie said, 'Well, that's the last of that for now, I hope.'

I said, 'Yeah.'

We both said good night.

I had a few more samey days of working. Then a new boy started, and I'm such a veteran after two and a half weeks, that Dale has me training him. Now this boy has very promising Guntheresque qualities. He is like baby Gunther. He has long blondy-red hair and little pointy incisors. Not as pronounced as

Gunther's, but he's sexy all right. Tall and thin.

His name is Neil and he's a damn lazy worker, but so pretty to look at. He just sort of hangs around me a lot, quietly, acting like he's listening to me talk about how Dale wants things done. Granted, a lot of the stuff I'm telling him is so trivial I'm embarrassed to be telling it. We've had a few laughs about that. Well, I did. He just kind of grinned sexily.

I remember lying in bed one of those nights after work (still missing Gunther, missing all our habits together...). But thinking new thoughts, as well. I was thinking how cool it would be to train up this new young Gunther. He is my own age after all. Or near enough. He could stay by my side as long as I told him to; he has no reason not to. And because he's younger, he wouldn't be so stubborn and set in his ways like Old Gunther. He wouldn't be driving off in the early dawn thinking he'd done right.

So my mind was made up, and I guess I must be a pretty determined person. Because the next day we were making out, out back by the spare microwave. The 'ring for service' bell was ringing, and it took me a while to register it. My senses were a little overstimulated, and that ringing in my ears was just another sensation. It was OK kissing Neil. He was kind of an erratic kisser. Not solid, like the farm boy. Not soft and lush like the punky one: kind of pushy, then vague, then pushy again all of a sudden. His Guntherisms added a touch of romantic excitement, though. And all those plans I had for him. Keeping those points in mind, it was nice to be kissing him.

Finally it dawned on me after who-knows-how-many seconds that that was the bell for service clamoring away up there. I jogged up to the counter, shouting, 'Can I help you?' as I went.

'I dunno, maybe you can.' It was Dale. 'Maybe you can tell me how to get some fucking service in this place!'

'Um.'

'Where the *heck* have you two been?'

Again, I was smooth under pressure. 'We were, I was, um, showing…Neil? The um…'

'You're a bad liar, missy! And if I catch either of the two of ya goofing off again, you're out on your pert little ass. And that goes for you, too.' He jerked his head toward Neil.

Neil replied brightly, 'I have a pert little ass?'

Dale bellowed, 'I don't like your attitude!'

Neil said, 'I don't like yours either.' Jeez, he didn't know when to quit.

Dale's head looked like his eyes were going to pop out like two buttons flying off an over-tight shirt. 'YOU'RE FIRED.'

Neil was out the door without so much as a glance at Dale or me. Dale turned to me. I was at my post on the other side of the counter, standing up straight, doing my best to appear the model of an attentive employee.

'And you,' Dale considered for a few seconds. 'You better watch yourself.'

I walked home later in the creepy suburban silence. There was only a sliver of moon, not putting out much light. I wondered if Gunther would ever act so hot-headed as Neil. Maybe in his hedonistic days. I wasn't sure. I was still keen on the idea of catching a young Gunther early; cementing our bond before he got so singular no one could stick to him.

I slept late, and when I got up I heard Stephanie on the phone. She was saying, 'She's fine. I'm fine. Yeah, yeah, I know…'

I burst in with, 'Is that Gunther?'

She spun and said, 'Hey, I better go.'

'Let me talk to Gunther.'

She was listening to something he was saying, and not handing me the phone.

'Let me talk to *fucking* Gunther!' I snatched the phone from her hand, brought it to my ear and lips, opened my mouth to say, 'Gunther'...Dial tone.

I was torn between the urge to let the receiver slide limply out of my hand and clunk to the floor, or smash it against the handset repeatedly, like some dime store punk. I still hadn't made up my mind when Stephanie took it out of my hand and hung it up for me.

I was hungry. I hadn't eaten when I got in the night before; I'd gone straight to bed. And I didn't have any snacks at work with Dale because I was in trouble. I didn't have any snacks before that because I was flirting with and subsequently kissing Neil. I slumped at the kitchen table while Stephanie made us some breakfast. Looked like she was making pancakes. She was in full housewife mode again this morning, which was usually cozy, but right then coziness couldn't touch me.

I felt like bursting into tears. I was chewing on my bottom lip. I could feel my face being drained of color, of blood. Then I wanted to run to my room screaming, baby tantrum style. But I do like to try and remain calm.

Stephanie looked over at me, frying pan in hand, and sighed a big sigh.

Given my emotional state and the weight of my feelings, it would have been fittingly dramatic to refuse all food. Part of me wanted to go all symbolic like that. But as I mentioned, I was damn hungry, and couldn't be bothered to muck around about it. I gobbled down my pancakes, then had seconds. I didn't talk, and didn't observe basic table manners, either. I grabbed at stuff without asking for it to be passed and slathered it on, ate too fast, let a mess of crumbs and syrup slide from my plate. I satisfied myself that this brutishness matched my thoughts on the matter perfectly.

At length Stephanie said, 'You know, he *really* cares about you. It's nice to have a friend like that.'

I was still chewing.

She said a few more things, and then, 'When you're older, you'll understand.'

Christ! I hate it when they say that. When I'm older, if I'm anything like the rest of them, I'll have lost the ability to understand anything. Her making that stupid statement is a case in point. Gunther was the only clear-thinking, straight-talking adult I'd come across, and now he was turning all muddly and hypocritical like the rest of them.

★

We've stayed out of each other's hair for a few days. I was working anyway. Neil stopped by work a couple of times. We kept moving our make-out spots. I guess that made us feel like we were exercising at least some caution. On the second night he had me tinglier than I'd ever been before. And then he just unzipped my pants, pushed my undies to one side and stuck it in. I'd noticed him doing a lot of fumbling around down there; I didn't actually register that he had his dick out, ready to launch an attack. It fucking hurt, and it was all I could do to keep from screaming. I thought it might get easier with time (I'd heard that), so I gritted it out. But waiting for it to hurt less was making me tenser.

Finally I let out an involuntary whimper, about the same time as he put it back in his pants and said, 'Aw, forget it.' Looked to me like he was already leaving, but he made a proper dash for it when we heard Dale coming in.

I made it to the counter in a flash, and stood face to face with Dale as the sound of the back exit slamming echoed through the store. I must have looked like hell. I had stuff running down the inside of my legs. This was just not a good time to have anyone staring at you.

He said, 'You're under probation.'

I went home and took a long bath. Stephanie and I got takeaway Chinese food. I stayed up watching an old black and white vampire movie, which eventually got too boring even for a vampire freak like me.

The next morning I walked into the kitchen and said, 'Steph, I wasn't gonna make a big fuss, but it's my birthday.'

I wasn't going to tell her, I didn't feel like drawing all that attention. But then I thought, 'Why am I being such a loser?'

Stephanie got worked up fast. 'What? Why didn't you tell me? I haven't—we could've—'

Ah, birthdays. Now I kind of did feel like doing something. Steph practically exploded, 'You're eighteen!'

We sat down with a pot of coffee and some blueberry muffins I'd brought home from work a couple of nights before. She stuck a candle in mine. Now anyone can see Stephanie and I don't have much in common, what with her being flaky and arty, and me more…realistic. But I like her kooky gestures.

She said, 'We'll do something later, OK?'

She has a new job teaching art to deaf people, or

something like that. She's been at it a couple weeks now, a few days per week.

I said, 'Yeah, cool.'

She told me to think of something I felt like doing.

I was still feeling pretty low key. I spent the morning doing not much, mostly on the couch. I don't know too many people in Steph's town. Truth be told, I don't feel like I live here at all. Naturally I feel like I belong back on the road with Gunther, back on track. After lunch I wandered down to the convenience store. Thought I might smooth things over with Dale, and look up Neil's number while I was there.

Dale looked pleasantly surprised to see me, and even more pleasantly surprised when I told him it was my birthday. I shuffled around and bought a few things. Then I asked if I could use the 'employee washroom'. He said yeah, of course.

Dale keeps a notebook out back there on the shelf, sort of an employee Rolodex. I stood in the storeroom and rifled through this. Man, he has poor handwriting. He hadn't gotten rid of Neil yet. He'd left his page intact with name, phone number, and allocated shifts. But he had scratched the word 'prick' across it, in his sprawling retarded script.

When I got home I dialed Neil. I thought it might be nice to get at least a couple of people together, to make an occasion of it, as me and Stephanie decided we would. I thought he might like to be included, now that we'd taken our relationship to the next level.

A husky voiced man answered, I assumed to be his dad. He bellowed through the house for Neil, who eventually answered.

'Yeah?'

I said, 'Hey.'

And he said, 'Hey...Who is this?'

When he heard it was me he said, 'Oh, hey' again.

'It's my birthday,' I blurted.

He said, 'Oh, well, happy—Have a good one.'

'Thanks, if you want to come over me and Stephanie are—'

He cut me off. 'No thanks.'

I said, 'Uh, OK.' And then, 'Why not?'

He started rambling a bit here. He said a few things, and then, 'Look just forget it, all right? Just...'

I asked him what I was supposed to be forgetting.

'You're not my *girlfriend*, all right,' he spat. 'Just leave me alone.'

This surprised me, and I was still thinking of something to say to make us behave a little nicer to each other when he hung up.

I went up to my room, lay down on my bed, and thought a while. It's always sad when people are jerks to you. But mostly I was sad that I hadn't located Baby Gunther after all. I had to go back to Plan A. I needed to find Gunther, or find a way to make him come back for me. I'd tried Vampire Prodigy Telepathy Mind Control. He didn't seem to get those messages.

I fantasized about being in some horrific accident, which would compel him to come back and sit by my hospital bed, filled with remorse. Maybe he would stroke my hand. Goodness knows he would fix those eyes on me.

Stephanie came home in kind of a state. I hoped it was just birthday excitement, but it was tinged with something else, a touch of the old raw Stephanie. And she had a bottle of Jim Beam in a brown paper bag.

She said, 'You know what?'

'What?'

'Gunther used to smoke with you, didn't he?'

'Yep.'

'And you handled yourself OK, didn't you?'

I said, 'Yep. Calmed me right down.'

'Well, I think we should have a drink. It's my house and I make the rules…Eighteen. God I was *shitfaced* when I turned eighteen! What do ya say to a birthday toast?'

I said, 'Sure.'

We went into the kitchen and sorted ourselves out with ice and Diet Coke. Then we sat back down on the lounge, with ample supplies of cola and bourbon within easy reach on the coffee table.

Steph raised her glass so high her arm was straight above her head. 'To birthdays,' she said. Then she added, 'To your birthday,' and patted me on the knee.

'Thanks,' I said, and clinked her glass way up there.

We had a few under our belts, and Steph was talking about stuff I had to do. Rites-of-passage sort of stuff. She'd been on the subject for a while, and I'd been pretty tight-lipped. But the drunker I got, the harder it was to withhold information; it became a crushing burden. The next time Steph came around to the subject of virginity I said, 'Steph, it's already happened.'

She said, 'What?'

I went, 'Yeah, the other night.' And added perkily, 'Someone just up and stuck it in.'

Steph yelled, 'I didn't even know you had a boyfriend!'

I said, 'Turns out I don't.'

We talked a little while about Neil, and I explained his similarities to Gunther.

She said, 'But those are only skin deep.'

'But he reminds me of him a lot.'

'Yes, but only physically. Gunther would have never treated you, I mean anyone, that way.'

'Not even in his hedonistic days?'

She paused and then smirked. 'No, not even when he was a bit more…freewheeling. Hon, he was still Gunther. He was still a good person.'

We paused and considered this for a moment.

Then I said, 'Jimmy.'

'What?'

'You know Jimmy.'

Steph said, 'Yeah, what about him?'

I said, 'I hate that dick.'

She looked pleased and amused.

Then I added, 'He's a dick,' just in case the point needed more emphasis.

The doorbell rang and Steph yelled, 'It's open!' And then jolted to attention and started hastily tidying our little table. By then we were both quite smashed, and it basically just involved herding the various pieces of incriminating evidence into a tighter, more symmetrical arrangement in the middle of the table. It reminded me of all the piles she had scattered around the house when we first got there.

A bunch of frumpy looking women marched into the room, all wearing prissy dresses, all looking completely appalled. It looked like someone had cloned a mother-in-law in various stages of development.

The old ugly one front and center snorted, 'Well, Stephanie! I just don't—what on earth do you call this?'

The younger one with red curly hair said, slightly more bashfully, 'We thought it might be nice to drop in on you.'

'Well, you could have called first.' Steph seemed kind of mad.

The old battleaxe was definitely mad. 'I *did* call first.'

Steph withered a bit. 'Oh, God, I totally forgot.' And then, 'Was that…when was that?'

I scooched closer to Stephanie on the couch, to make more room in case they wanted to sit down. That just made matters worse. Now I think they thought we were lesbians, because the old bitch took in the scene afresh and gasped, 'Oh, *Stephanie*.'

I stayed put. Hell, I didn't care if they thought we were having some girl-on-girl action. I've never seen anything wrong in that. A lot of girls are damn pretty, I can see that. And apart from Gunther, a lot easier to talk to than boys. Not that I'm experienced or anything, I just don't have a problem with it. I don't have a problem with lots of things.

Gunther and I were on the subject once, and he called me 'delightfully broad-minded', which he said is a great asset to me, as long as I keep my feet on the ground, or at least one foot on the ground. He gave me a happy iceberg-eyed shimmer. I said what about all those crazy times of his, and he said he was grounded. That riled me up. I'm grounded. I may muse about him being a vampire half the time, but how is he to know that? Unless he can read minds…

Back in the living room I was asked how old I was, and replied, 'Twenty-three.'

Then the rough formation of disgusted women turned on their heels and left. Steph looked flat. Really flat.

She said, 'My late husband's sister.' Then added, her voice breaking, 'And some ladies from *church*.'

I said, 'I didn't know you go to church.'

She said, 'I don't. I didn't!'

'Oh, Stephanie,' I just wanted to get our party going again. 'You're entitled to live it up a little.'

She put her head in her hands and burst out sobbing. I gave her some weak pats on the shoulder. Then I got up and started to clear up, and realized I was too drunk. We both fell asleep there on the couch.

I woke up early, feeling like my head was a balloon about to pop. I'd thrown up on myself a little. Steph was still out cold. I got up and took a shower.

When I got back to the living room, with my wet hair and my clean clothes, feeling slightly less like shit, Steph was still there. She was just beginning to unfold herself from her curled-up position into a more vertical one. She moved a few bottles and things around on the coffee table, then she looked up at me and said, 'Hair of the dog?'

I said, 'Um…OK.'

I had been expecting her to swing back into Good Stephanie housewife mode. I thought having those angry broads crashing in on her might have given her a shock. Enough of one to send her back into the safe haven of decent living.

I think she was still drunk. We sat on the front porch with a couple of glasses and polished off the rest of the bourbon, which was mostly just backwash. Stephanie had started swigging from the bottle toward the end of the night.

Doing that, sitting there, was a good vantage point to survey all that suburban crispness. There was something satisfying about it. Everything else around us was afraid to stir. And when it did stir, it just let out a predictable little peep. A garage door opening and closing, a bird chirping. I felt like a couple of hillbillies. She was sitting in a rocking chair. At the same time, feeling like a blight on a landscape like that made me feel urbane and pretty cool.

We sat out there for a while, quietly and meaningfully sipping, although every swallow of lukewarm Jim Beam made my throat burn. It wasn't going down too easy, and I was strongly considering abandoning the attempt. But I have a bit of the old Gunther Shared Ritual in me, I think.

Then old Jimmy came crashing into his yard, thunderously revving his pick-up, bucking-bronco style, before skidding it to a dead stop directly in front of us. Stephanie, to complete the demure suburban cliché, lived in a cul de sac. We were right at the end, so her yard curved toward his. And naturally Jimmy drove a shiny black pick-up truck. What the hell else would he drive? Of course he parked it out on the front lawn. He shot us a filthy sideways glance and headed inside, screen door slamming behind him.

Stephanie cleaned herself up and went to work. I went to work. It seemed things were back to normal.

She was sitting on the couch watching TV, eating rice crackers, when I got home. She said she'd been out on a date. She met this guy at work, Phillip. He sounded nicer than Jimmy. Or at least I thought he should be, since she met him at a nice person's job, doing nice person things. Helping the underprivileged to enjoy themselves more, and suchlike.

I went to my room and thought about Gunther some more. I was certain he could feel our connection; how the distance between our minds formed a straight, unbreakable line between us. I knew he could feel me there, wherever he was, thinking about him. I couldn't entertain the thought that he didn't feel me, couldn't feel me; wasn't thinking of me at all. That was too terrifying. Did I mention he left me the typewriter? And a stack of grade-A recycled typing paper.

The next day I left for work early, and wandered around town. I passed a boy sitting in a doorway who gave me little puppy dog eyes. He was cute, and I knew he was giving me the green light. He was looking at me like I could help him fix a problem. Looked like he needed saving, or at least some friendly company. But I didn't even break stride.

It's not the same without Gunther. It doesn't seem as adventuresome. When he was out having his night, and I was out having mine, we were still linked, due to reconvene. Sometimes I really did feel like two vampires out on the feed. Out there in the night, kissing boys was safer *and* more thrilling. Gunther was my anchor, and I was out swimming on a line.

Things have been boring for a while with me working, Stephanie working, her dating, and me not being in the mood for boys. I'm saving up money, but I'm still not sure what to do with it.

★

Phillip came over for dinner, after those two had been dating a few weeks. I had the night off, and they said I could stay put. Well, Stephanie did, and Phillip concurred. He said I could call him Phil. She was making grilled fish with various side dishes, and going to a lot of effort.

He said, 'Mmmm, something smells good.'

They drank white wine and talked about work. He gave her plenty of advice on people and things. I guess he'd been working there a lot longer. Steph seemed to be taking it all in. She tapped the wine bottle and raised an eyebrow in my direction. I shook my head in a quick secretive jerk. Phillip seemed square as all hell, and I didn't want to bring down Stephanie's rep.

But then she did it herself in a matter of seconds. She regaled him with the finer points of our night of sanctioned under-age drinking. The horrible old hens crashing in on us, the rites-of-passage speeches, laughing away. She didn't seem to notice his look of brow-furrowing concern.

I thought, 'Man, Steph is such a ditz sometimes.' So I said, 'It was my idea.' Then, 'Steph was already drunk.'

We all sat there in tense silence. I think Phillip

actually clucked his tongue; think I saw him shake his head. Then I thought, 'Crud. I am a feeble fucking excuse-maker.'

'Stephie, I don't think that sounds right,' he said finally.

Christ. Why do they all call her 'Stephie'?

She said, 'Yeah you're probably right.' Then added softly, 'She's older than she…seems.'

'And now, I don't think that makes sense.' He peered meaningfully into her eyes. He has brashly blue 'I'm a rugged yet sensitive guy' eyes that are somewhat piercing. Hers are warm brown. By this point he had summoned enough dripping earnestness to add, '…Do you?'

I got up and sat on the couch, turned on the TV. The living room shares a doorway with the kitchen; I could still see them in there. Stephanie was washing the dishes, and Phillip was standing behind her rubbing her shoulders. Really, he was more just grabbing her shoulders, holding her there. He shot me a couple of sidelong glances. He was telling her she was a nice lady, and shouldn't let herself be manipulated by a kid like me.

I was still miffed the next morning. Stephanie and I shuffled around awkwardly and didn't say much to each other. I ate too much breakfast and lay around on the couch like a beached whale. There was an extremely authoritative knock on the front door.

I thought, 'Jeez, there's no need to knock like a cop.'

Apparently there was. It was a cop.

He said, 'Afternoon, miss.'

I said, 'Morning.'

He said, 'I've heard reports of some underage drinking going on here. Would you know anything about that?'

I said, 'No…sir, I…Stephanie occasionally has a…nightcap, but I don't join her.'

'Stephanie. That's the lady of the house?'

'Yes.'

'Is she at home?'

'I'm right here.' Stephanie came marching in looking put out and determined.

'Ma'am, I've heard accounts of underage drinking here. You wouldn't be supplying liquor to a minor by any chance, would you?'

Stephanie said pleasantly, 'Now, we did have a toast the other night, because it was her birthday—'

'I had root beer!' I shouted.

The cop kept his attention directed at Stephanie.

'Are you this child's legal guardian?'

'I'm her…She is under my care.'

He leaned over me. 'Would you say you're being well looked after?'

I said yes, and he said he'd be in touch.

Naturally this exchange stressed us out, but we didn't have time to talk about it until that night, when we'd both got home from work. We were cursing whoever turned us in.

Stephanie said it must have been the uptight 'well-wishing' bitches. (One of them had actually left a card, propped up on the television. It read, *I deeply feel your loss* against a background of sunset pink.)

'Or Jimmy,' I said. 'He gave us a funny look.'

'Yeah,' she mused, 'he's probably bearing a grudge.'

'Or Phillip!' I chimed.

'What?'

'Why not?'

'Phillip's a very nice man.'

'Oh, c'mon Stephanie. Phillip would rat us out and act like he was doing us a favor.'

She got pretty crotchety. 'He's the nicest man I've been out with in quite some time,' she said.

I was fixing to say, 'That's not saying much,'

but thought better of it. For one thing, it mightn't be true. Her late husband Ward was probably nice; Gunther had said as much.

We chugged our hot chocolates and went to our respective beds. I did my usual pine for Gunther. This was my nightly ritual, the way some people say prayers. I dropped off to sleep, and slept half the next day away. I missed Stephanie leaving for work, and nearly missed leaving for work myself.

It was funny how Stephanie could get the cops called 'round for drinking backwash on her own porch, while Gunther could sit out there passing joints back and forth with me like no one's business. God I miss that self-made renegade. How he's gracefully expanded beyond the confines of acceptable living, pushed past the walls of that box that most people cower inside. Was he ever stuck in there at all? It's hard to imagine.

Dale was damn chatty that night. I was too grumpy to offer much in the way of responses, but he didn't seem to notice. If anything, he liked it better that way. Maybe he liked talking to an employee and not having to scan their replies for sarcasm.

Stephanie was in bed when I got home. The next day she told me Phillip had vouched for her respectability. She'd already told him about the cop dropping by. So by the time the cop found the gall to go sniffing around her work, Phillip was all ready to be her knight in shining armor. He sent the pig packing, with an impassioned tirade which combined a nod to Stephanie's upstandingness with a lamentation on the breakdown of civil liberties. It sounded like quite a performance; Stephanie was visibly moved.

He came around for dinner again, too soon for my liking. He asked us if we'd learned our lesson, playing with fire like that. He said he hoped we had, and that sometimes you had to learn things the hard and fast way. Then he dribbled on about something his grandfather had taught him; tough love and all that. And I thought, 'This nutball turned us in.'

He gave Stephanie one of those looks again, across the table.

'So we've had enough excitement for a while. Hmmm, Peachy?'

Peachy? When did that start? It's a bit early for pet names. I had lots of things running through my head. Gunther likes me to respect my elders, but he also doesn't mind me getting feisty now and again.

I said, 'Anything would be too much excitement

for you,' as I pushed my chair out from under me and left the room.

Later that night, after Phillip left and Stephanie had done all her little chores, she came and sat next to me.

She said, 'I don't know why you're trying to fuck this up for me.' She peered at me and said, '*Are* you trying to fuck this up for me?'

I was at a loss and just stared at her.

She went on, 'I really like this guy, and I don't know if you're jealous, or what, but…Don't fuck this up for me.'

I was still stuck for words. I hadn't been this disgusted with Stephanie for a long time. For one thing, I couldn't see what the success or failure of her lame relationship, a mere link in her chain of bad relationships, had to do with me. But more to the point, and this I decided to share:

'He's a dick, Stephanie.'

'What? How could—he is not!'

Now I was in the thick of it. She shouted, 'Why you insolent little—you *are* jealous!'

That jealousy stuff was really cranking my shaft, and I hit her with, 'What, do you have to be drunk to listen to reason?'

She gave me a withering fiery glare. I just sat there. I imagined two little lasers, boring into my flesh. Then I mumbled, almost apologetically, 'He's just as much a dick as Jimmy, just in a different way.'

I figured we were done talking and banished myself to my room. But I kept the train of thought. That night was one long meditation on dickishness, which I picked up again in the morning. I woke up, got ready, and headed for the door, thinking, 'God, they really are all dicks. Gunther is the only non-dick.'

But then, where the hell is he? Abandoning someone you supposedly care about, who cares about you tons, without so much as a word…His lame fucking disappearing act—Gunther's just as much a dick as the rest of them.

No sooner had I thought this, when I opened the front door to see him standing on the porch. He had a sheepish but very self-possessed grin on his face. I stared up at him in all his tallness, with the sun behind him. He looked like Jesus on a fucking cloud. If Jesus were a lanky vampire. It was blinding.

I packed my bag and grabbed the typewriter. I didn't bother telling work I wouldn't be in today, or ever again. I wasn't sure if Gunther had spoken to Stephanie. I didn't care. I planted myself in the passenger seat as quickly as I could.

I was quiet for a minute, just breathing in the relief of being back on the road.

Then I said, 'I have lots of money now, Gunther.'

And then, 'Where the fuck have you been?'

He grinned just faintly enough to show a hint of fang. I didn't really care where he'd been. Now he was back.

He asked, 'Did you and Stephanie have fun?'

I said, 'Stephanie's a pain in the ass.' Then I mumbled, 'We had our moments, I guess.'

He grinned wider.

We did our usual, passing through towns, stopping at diners. I just filled my eyes with Gunther. I'd pictured our reunion over and over back at Stephanie's. I was nearly always giving him a big serve, and he was almost always remorseful. But now I found I wasn't mad at all. All Gunther's disappearance and reappearance served to do was bowl me over with how crazy glad I was to see him. God, the sun is shining down on me, on us, again.

I wonder if he knows I'm legal now. Because I've been doing a lot of thinking.

★

We holed up in a hotel room and passed our first reunited evening in the customary joint-rolling and smoking fashion. I hadn't smoked in a while. We talked a little, but it was all such a dream. I fell into a deep sleep without even noticing.

I was pretty groggy the next morning, but slotted quickly back into the old morning processes. We did all our individual getting ready stuff, and packed the car. Gunther had half a trunk full of grade-A recycled paper. I had to move two newish looking typewriter ribbons off my seat. I sort of giggled. 'What am I writing, War and Peace?'

He answered, 'I don't know. Maybe,' and started the engine.

Gunther has his stubborn air of mystery about him, as always. I mean, for an open guy, for someone who draws chosen people in close, he still has his distinct limits. Probing is nearly always fruitless, and feeling like a pest hurts my pride. I don't like the sensation of him reeling away, so I try not to cross his lines. I wait for him to come to me. Unless we're stoned and joking around. All's fair in drugs and war! I once shouted that at him, whilst jumping on a hotel bed. It wasn't quite a rooftop, but who else did I need to tell?

So I wasn't too bothered about asking him where he'd been and why. It was just Gunther stuff, I'm sure. But he asked a bit about me and Stephanie. I told him some of the ups and downs. Gunther thinks I'm smart, and he thinks I 'get people'. He didn't think I was off in left field when I declared Stephanie's men dicks. He figured I had my reasons, which I did. I asked him what Ward was like. He said he was serious.

Gunther never gets stoned during the day. It's an evening indulgence. Occasionally I imbibe in the daylight hours, on long quiet stretches of road, much to his chagrin. When we drove past a sign to the Grand Canyon I was so stoned I thought it said, 'The Grand Crayon'. It was all infectious giggles from there. I said, 'Hey Gunther, we should go look at that.'

He said, 'We should.'

So we did. We both stood there, looking out. But he spent most of that time looking at me. I could see his warm, glinty-toothed smirk out of the corner of my eye.

After a while, when we were on the road again, I said, 'Gunther?'

'Yeah?'

'If we're driving past the Grand…Crayon!… does that mean we're heading east again?'

'Mmm, basically.'

'I thought we were going to California.'

'Well, which coast did you want? They both have their good points.'

'Um?'

'What do you say to New York City?'

'Um, yeah, sure.' Then I thought about it and yelled, 'Did you go to San Francisco without me?'

He actually stammered for a few seconds. 'Well I, not as…' Then regained his composure with a gleeful, 'Bit young to be a ball and chain, aren't you?'

We stopped in a sun-drenched hicky township, to grab a bite in what looked to be an old-style saloon, give or take a few hookers. Gunther was at the bar talking to the proprietor. There was a young precocious country bumpkin hanging around, and she and I got to talking.

'Is he your husband?' she asked.

I couldn't believe I'd accomplished the huge leap from alleged daughter to wife.

'No…'

'That guy is hot.'

'Think so?'

'Fucking hot.'

An impromptu heart to heart ensued, during which she told me to jump his bones. She said old guys never make the first move. No one wants to be a dirty old man. But no one wants to be a lonely old man, either. I told her I thought Gunther liked being a lonely old man. She said loving each other's the best thing a couple of people can do. She finished on a romantic high with, 'Shit, fucking's about the *only* thing a coupla people can do in this boring shithole,' then mumbled, 'New York City. Wish I had your luck...'

Personally, I don't see the rush in regard to nailing Gunther. For one thing, I haven't really properly done it yet. That hasty puncture wound out back of the convenience mart barely counted. I don't know what I'm missing yet; have nothing to long for. I can feel a building desire to be closer to him, though. I am comfortably certain he is the man for me. I hate to think of him wanting me too, yet hanging back over some tortured confliction. I don't want him to suffer. And then there is the whole potential Soulmates of Eternal Darkness thing. I'm up for that.

★

It's nice just to be chatting again. That night, over our joints, I told him about losing my virginity. He listened somberly, then said it was about as unromantic as his first time. He asked if the experience had any redeeming qualities. I said no, not really. I didn't want to tell him the only plus was envisioning I was with a younger him. I feel so many things for Gunther that it didn't seem that pressing to come over all slutty. He told me his first time was with a prostitute.

'What, really?'

'Yes, I just thought it was about time.'

'So, what, you saved up your allowance?'

'No, nothing like that.' He laughed. 'I haven't paid for it since, and I don't think I thought paying for it was such a hot idea back then, either. It just happened, as things do. Or it just occurred to me to let it happen.'

He paused. I passed him the joint. We were sitting on the bed, side by side, propped up by pillows. He resumed: 'I was having a dud of a night in this seedy bar, with my father, who was playing cards all night. And there was this lady, having a worse night than me, getting hit on by all these festy old assholes, knowing she'd have to close the deal with one of them. I'd just had a birthday—'

'How old?'

'Sixteen. She asked me, and at the time it felt like we were helping each other out.'

'Yeah.'

'And I was just a curious kid.'

He handed the joint back my way. 'But I can't imagine a more unromantic encounter. She may as well have been riding one of those amusement park carousel horses.'

'Was she pretty?'

'She was pretty old, as well. But, you know, that was OK.'

It was nearly the end of the joint, and our fingers touched in the handover. That was always a lovely sensation, stoned.

We fell asleep, clothes on, atop the covers. Well, he did. I lay there for a while listening to his breathing, wondering how he had ever found it in his heart to part us for all those tortured weeks.

The next day found us smack in the middle of the shadowless desert. We'd stopped at a remote fast food takeaway called Yogo's, with tacky little tables bolted to the ground outside at the base of a fifty foot Y, also bolted. This place sold postcards of local wildlife. Actually, I think they sold postcards of random wildlife. Because I don't think they have all those animals out there in the desert. Unless there was a zoo nearby. Pandas? I found one with a picture of an antelope with huge brown don't-hurt-me eyes.

I wrote:

hey Stephanie,

Sure is good to be back on the road. You'll be glad to hear I'm not grumpy anymore. Feel like myself again. This card reminds me of you.

xx

Freedloader

We were on our way to see another of Gunther's friends. But taking it a bit slower this time. This guy Maurice lives in the middle of someone else's farm. He's renting a delightful little shack out here, all full of knick-knacks and whimsical clutter. What a motor-mouthed whirlwind he is. It's a wonder how he exists out here with barely anyone to talk to. Maybe he saves it up.

We've been here a day and a half, and he sure is doing his best to ensure my visit is educational. I got a tour of all the surrounding plantlife, which included farm crops, and weeds, among other more exotic varieties.

He plays violin, quite beautifully. And sings baritone. After dinner he brought his violin onto the front porch and regaled us with his own lilting, masterful compositions, echoing out over all the deaf nothingness.

In the morning he explained to me why it was so beneficial to drink one's first urine of the day. Apparently it contains the most nutrients of any other urine you might pass throughout the day. Good for just about anything that ails you. He actually managed to be quite convincing.

After a few days I was sure Maurice was a wise man. I asked him if he thought Gunther and I loved each other.

'Has he been keeping his distance?'

'Yes,' I said.

'Sumptuous little critter like you…Well, then, yes I would say it is likely.'

This was somewhat pondersome, but I took it to mean I was in with a chance. I don't think I've been called a critter before. I definitely haven't been called sumptuous.

Maurice tends a small, scattered crop of opium poppies (these were part of the tour). He 'milked' them, and scaped this onto a cigarette paper; basically buttered it. Gunther and I headed off with some of these, and rolled them into joints that night in our hotel. What a beautiful place to be that room was. Wrapped in all our slowly drifting smoke, rising like dragon's breath over guarded jewels, countless riches. Opium joints are a dreamier stone, and it was all I could do to stay away from him.

I said, 'Sometimes you're just too far away,' as I pulled him toward me by his arm. I kissed him. 'I like you.'

'I like you, too,' he said, in an utter daze, and kissed me back.

This wasn't anything like any of the other kissing. It was slow and hypnotic, and utterly thrilling. We could pause over each other's mouths, lips only brushing, just breathing. He could run his cheek over mine, cat style, so all I could feel was his warm breath, the tickle of his eyelashes. And then there was the deeper kissing, with tongues.

We just got on a roll with all this, and went all the way. I couldn't have imagined doing anything else. Just melted into it. Not bad for the second time. Now I could definitely see why everyone liked it so much. And why Gunther's women never had much to complain about. He did all sorts of cool stuff to me. And apparently sex can last a lot longer. He said he'd build up some longevity for me, it'd just been a while for him…I wasn't one to complain. I fell asleep in his arms, and when we woke up, we did it again. He kissed me a lot. We made our way to the shower together. He even washed me. And kissed me some more.

I didn't know it would be like that. I thought it might be a little strange after all that time of friendship, touching each other like that; a little awkward, maybe. I didn't know I wouldn't be able to stop touching him, that it would feel like I was attached to marionette strings, that I was being constantly drawn to him, through no conscious will of my own. I would snap to, and find myself holding his hand, or clutching my arms around his waist, like a sleepwalker. Lovewalker.

It was such a relief to finally bask in our feelings

for each other. Every notion I had ever entertained about Gunther and me opened up before us, hovering in an attractive collection of possibilities. Even the concept of forging an eternal pact as creatures of the night enjoyed increased plausibility. I was as happy as a clam.

He said a funny thing, though, first thing in the morning as he unwrapped his arms from me. He said I surprised him, that he would have envisioned himself waking up a little more…alone.

We had a day of us being close, of touching each other and not being able to help it. We got some looks, but those look-givers couldn't reach me. I'd found a way to transport that safe bubble of perfect happiness everywhere we went. It was the stoned hotel-room feeling, times a thousand. More, even.

There was more smoking and slow kissing that night. Gunther stopped and held me for a while. He said just the touch of me made him feel at ease. I told him it was nice to be that close to him.

I'd heard people get skin-hungry. People can actually get depressed if they're not touched enough; single people, old people and the like. My grandmother told me that. And I've often thought about it, because I was never touched much as a child.

So there is the comfort. But there is also an electricity to Gunther and my touching. His hand sliding down my arm carries a charge. And caressing him back, that carries a charge, too. Putting our hands together, lining up the fingertips, that is a major conductor. I'd heard you can do that by yourself; that turning your palms to face each other and holding your fingertips together harnesses kinetic energy. Imagine what two people can do.

I got all excited again, and we ended up going all the way, again.

He didn't hold me all night that time, and he was up on the phone in the morning. We were rushing off to see another friend of his. We got on the road pretty quick. We held hands a bit during the day, but when we got to his friend's he said he'd like to just 'keep it to ourselves' for now.

This friend, Stan, lives right on the edge of suburbia; his yard borders a huge pine forest, which is cool. He has a son my age, just a little younger. Eight months, we worked out. Leopold, which is a weird name for someone around my age, but OK if you call him Leo, which everyone does. He's nice.

I must be following Gunther around too much, because Stan laughed and said, 'Why don't you go and play with someone your own age?'

And things between Gunther and me must be kind of obvious, because later Stan clapped him on the back and said, 'You old dog.'

Gunther can't have been very pleased with that. He's really more of a cat. This was the first time I'd ever seen him look ashamed of himself. Now that we were finally happy. What a crazy world.

Leo has a blond and fragile look about him. With a dash of Tom Sawyer thrown in, maybe because he lives so close to those wild woods. We went exploring. I reckon he's had a crush on me from the word go. As if I'd ever cheat on Gunther.

Gunther has two friends around these parts. This other friend, Emily, who lives a couple of towns over, has been pestering him to come visit for a while. He'd told me a while back it was going to be potentially awkward. He thought she may have romantic inclinations toward him, and wasn't sure they were reciprocal. At the time I thought this was a subtle hint in my direction, that maybe he carried a torch for me. And here I thought putting the moves on him had cleared all this up, because he could just bring me along. She would see he was spoken for, and that would be that.

Gunther and I have had a few days of separateness at Stan and Leo's; separate bedrooms, separate daily activities. But I'm not too bothered about this. We have cemented enough of a connection to keep me going for a while.

Leo and I were going to go on a long hike, through the forest, out the other side, to look at Leo's mother's grave. I thought that sounded like a good expedition, and invited Gunther along. He declined, and said he was heading out to Emily's later.

I said, 'Oh. For how long?'

'I'm booked for the next few days,' was his curt reply.

Now I know how he likes his own space, and we're still friends, after all. So I just said, 'OK.'

Leo and I headed out on our walk by ourselves. I've been telling him bits and pieces about me and Gunther. I'm just too happy to keep it to myself. Also, I need Leo to understand why I won't be kissing him and stuff, even though he is pretty cute. We walked for about half an hour, then sat down on a log in a clearing.

Leo said, 'You know Gunther's gonna bone that Emily?'

'What?'

'I heard him bragging to my dad. Gonna be a holiday romance, he said.'

'He doesn't even like her.'

Leo laughed. 'He likes the idea of making sweet, sweet love to her.' Then he added, more tenderly, 'Personally, I think he's crazy, if you guys have True Love.'

I nearly jogged to Leo's mom's grave. I stood there for what I thought seemed a polite allotment of time to stand graveside. Then I basically ran back.

Leo was panting and sweating up a storm, and said, 'Sheesh, you're fit.'

I heard Gunther's car. I caught up with him halfway down the driveway, banged on the passenger side door. There wasn't any sharp-toothed grinning. He looked very flustered to see me. I leaned in the window.

'Gunther, Leo says this trip to Emily's is gonna be a total fuckfest.'

Gunther looked exasperated.

I added hopefully, 'I figure he's just messing with my head...'

He said, 'Look, I can't talk about this now, and I really just want to get on the road.'

I said, 'OK,' but must have looked extremely

unimpressed. He was giving me the sort of lame brush-off I could accept from the Neils of the world; from Gunther, it was a little harder to take.

He softened, but not enough to resemble the Gunther I knew, and launched into a lengthy ramble about how he hates to hurt people. Last week he had been fancy free, he said. He had this encounter with Emily on the horizon, which was cleanly devoid of consequences. No one stood to get hurt. (She just wanted a quick bang or two, by the sounds, which he was only too happy to provide.) He said he was powerless to refuse women at their most vulnerable. Hated to romantically crush them. Gunther said he might be the only free-spirited rogue this chick knew. (Since when was he a rogue? I thought he was a pseudo-celibate vampire, saving himself for a love like mine. That blew me out a bit.) Now he had her, who he cared for, and me, who he cared for, each a potential victim of his manly ability to draw pain. Hence his policy of minimal involvement.

Then he made a bumpy segue onto the subject of our age difference. He talked about an old pervert or two he'd witnessed over time and said, 'I don't want to be that guy.'

I actually figured he'd feel sort of that way. Even

I was slightly funny with it, but in my eyes our perfect love dwarfed all petty concerns and social mores.

I wanted him to calm down a bit. I said, 'Yeah, I guess I can see why you might feel that way. It's not like that didn't occur to me.'

'Yeah.' He did seem calmer. 'Well, I better go. I'll see you when I get back. Sunday at the latest.'

I said, 'OK.'

Well, that certainly turned my world upside down. I stayed calm until Leo came up and patted my shoulder, asking what was wrong. I ran to my room and cried a lot. Then I cleaned myself up for dinner. I wondered if Gunther was coming back, or if he was going to do another disappearing act. It was clear I'd spooked him.

He's been gone almost a week. During this time I've done enough meditating, from enough different angles, to have possibly achieved nirvana. There was the initial feeling of betrayal, offset by the sheer cruelty of the timing: I had only just entered a blissful state, only just gotten up the nerve and made the decision to bag Gunther. There was the shame of being made to look like a young hussy who'd thrown myself at him. There was the realization that I must feel more for him than he does for me. But I knew that couldn't be entirely true because of all the magic between us, and cursed him for being a coward. For running from the genuine to the trivial. For staring down our love in all its purity, and giving it the finger. Surely it must be over now. I'd make the announcement upon his return.

It was during this extended train of thought that Leo and I really began to bond. Let's face it; I was rebounding. We spent a few nights in my room, kissing and hugging. Then he'd go back to his, to avoid getting caught out by Stan.

It was nice to have a channel for my desire for closeness, which has risen exponentially since first touching Gunther. On the third night I let him go all the way with me. It was all right. But he just wasn't Gunther. And I was still thinking.

It occurred to me that if I really love Gunther the way I think I do, that I have to love *him*. And this is him. This silly jerk dashing off to possibly fuck this other chick. Otherwise I was just kidding myself; I didn't love him at all. I thought of all the times I'd disappointed people, all the people who wanted me to be something I wasn't, who took their love away.

Then I thought of all the people who I didn't want much to do with, like the farm boy, for example. What if he'd wanted to get all serious together. I wouldn't be into that. Then there was the type who robotically projects their own desires onto someone else. I don't want to be that person, the same way Gunther doesn't want to be the ageing pervert. The confused old fool; he's only trying to be true to himself. We are supposed to be free spirits. There isn't much free-spiritedness in trying to ensnare someone. Maybe we can still be on this crazy adventure together after all, we just need to sort a few things out.

By the time he got home, after exactly one week, I was ready for him. As luck would have it, Stan and Leopold were out on an overnight fishing trip. I'd stayed home with a 'headache'. Gunther came home and sat on my bed. I didn't ask him about Emily. I didn't want to know, couldn't speak her name. It was done now, and here we were. He rolled us some joints and we smoked them.

After about a joint and a half he asked if I was angry about him visiting her. I said no, I wasn't angry about that. I was angry that he acted like it was his moral duty to fuck her, and if he didn't he was a bad friend, which was somehow my fault.

He said, 'I don't know about moral duty.'

I still didn't want to know. We smoked some more. We decided to go downstairs and watch some TV. Eventually we wound up leaning together, just brushing. His touch was still his touch. We found each other's hands. Before I knew it I was kissing him again. There was still the element of safety, of slow, lingering, celebratory closeness. I had feared that would be lost. There was a little less of it this time, more of an edge, possibly the knowledge that this glitch hadn't killed us. This thing between us seemed to have a force of its own. Could it be stopped at all? I pulled him in closer and closer. I sucked his bottom lip into my mouth; I felt I could swallow him, drag him in even deeper; meld. He got his fangs onto my lip and held them there and nipped me, until I was forced to laughingly relinquish my grasp.

He asked me if I wanted to go to bed. I said yes, I did.

We curled up facing each other. It was such a relief, the most natural feeling in the world to be encased in that closeness again, with him.

I said, 'You didn't think it was such a bad thing when you had that older woman.'

'No, not really.'

'So what difference does it make if it's the girl who's the youngest?'

'Well…'

'Are you a sexist, Gunther?'

And by the heavens, I got a glinty-toothed grin. 'No, I am not a sexist.'

I got on top for the first time ever. He had to ask me to slow down. Then he told me I could speed up again. Then he laughed.

We had ourselves respectable again by the time Leo and Stanley came home. Gunther was frying up some bacon, and I was in the living room reading a home decorating magazine. They all had some bacon. I'm pseudo vegetarian. I find it hard to eat any animal I've actually bonded with. I know I'm a softy. And it's an odd position for someone who would consider sucking the blood of humans as a future lifestyle option. But, you know, you've got to follow your calling…

We left that afternoon. Leo tried to stop me, grabbed my sleeve in the hallway. We nearly had a tug of war with my bag. His face contorted into a ridiculous exaggerated grimace. He looked like one of those tribal masks. He seemed at a loss for words, and only grunted.

Finally he managed: 'Stupid old jerk.'

Bearing in mind I don't have a poker face, at all, I must have shot him a very filthy look. He changed his tack.

'I love you!'

Now that is something Gunther and I have never said to each other. Doesn't seem to be much point. It's so damn obvious; love is everywhere, surging around us, sweeping us up in its awe-inspiring near-religious fervor. What the hell is the point of chattering? It sounded so trivial coming from Leo I was almost insulted.

'Look, just give it up, OK?' I wrenched my sleeve from his grasp so abruptly I nearly fell backwards.

His face was contorting even more, as if that was possible. Jeez, it's not like he doesn't know Gunther and I are made for each other. I told him all that stuff, before we ever started fumbling around. Leo seemed to be operating under the assumption he had more action coming his way from me, and making a damn scene about it.

'Don't be a jerk,' were my parting words.

'Bitch,' was his.

Then he burst into tears. Proper baby sobs.

As Gunther bounced the car down their rocky driveway I asked, 'How can someone say they love you and then call you a bitch?'

He raised his eyebrows. He appeared to be forming an answer. Then he stopped and looked about to laugh. He finished off distant and brooding. That was more expressions than he usually makes in a day. He never did answer. And I didn't press him. I had a hunch I had asked something stupid.

We drove a little ways in silence. I thought about Leo from a clinical distance—far greater than the few miles we'd covered since his house…So now I can say I made a boy cry. I wonder if that is like being a vampire. Dipping into the world of the living, taking a nibble, ripping off a piece, no bigger than you need. Making someone bleed, then retreating to the solace of your own kind, your own darkness. Leo was so tiny, shrinking into the background. And Gunther and I, growing, enormous. I turned to face the driver's side. There was a puffy cloud-filled blue sky filling all the car windows. And Gunther, framed in all that brightness, calmly glaring down the road in front of us. That's Gunther, larger than life.

It was a relief to have him to myself again. I'd been looking forward to the smoking session in our room. Back to normal. Plus there was all the other stuff we did now. But now here he'd left me alone in the room with the precious typewriter, babysitter. He rolled a joint and walked outside onto the landing with it. I was reading some existentialist crap, and looked up around the time he should've handed the joint over to me. Seems he'd wandered off.

I waited a while and then went downstairs to see if I could find him. As I passed the front desk the manager said, 'Miss? Message for you.'

He handed me an envelope. It was fairly thick and chunky. It had the room number scrawled on it in Gunther script. I was filling with dread.

I walked back across the parking lot toward the room, opening it as I went. It was filled with money, a lot of money by my standards. I couldn't tell how much, a few hundred maybe. My eyes were filling with tears.

I couldn't believe Gunther'd left all that cash lying around with the greasy manager. He had a filthy undershirt and a wet comb-over. Some people seem to think hot weather justifies the absence of any and all fashion sense. That was an affront to common decency, which I'm sure Gunther must have observed. He clearly wasn't thinking straight. Oh fuck, fuck, fuck.

I got back to the room and had a hasty but thorough look around. He'd left all of his stuff. What a complete asshole he's being. He'll have to come back for it. I'll just wait. In hindsight I can't believe I didn't hear the old clunker revving up and pulling out of the lot. Gunther's car definitely has a major presence. But then, a close personal friend spontaneously bailing on you in the middle of a joint is not customarily something you listen out for. Bastard.

I sat around in the room some more, up on the huge double bed. I watched a game show. But I wasn't really watching, of course, I was thinking.

Gunther is clearly confused, I thought. And he hasn't really pretended otherwise. He hadn't pinned any notes to my chest, or left any otherwise conspicuously placed, so he must not have formulated an explanation for this departure. His stuff was here, so it must be temporary. Either that, or he was in that much of a hurry to get away from me. Because, why leave the money if he was coming right back? But I guess leaving the money shows that he does care about me; cares what happens to me, how I get by. I know he probably thinks he's bad for me, being so much older and all.

When I thought about it, I'd always put all the moves on him. Sometimes we'd sort of wind up brushing against each other, as I've mentioned before. But it was always me who sealed the deal. I would pull him toward me, or slide in closer, or take his hand, his arm, a leg. Sometimes I just had to kiss him. It couldn't be helped. That must have made it hard for him to exercise his Gunther restraint and distance. Guys just can't resist the advances of us young chicks, I'm told.

That must be why he once said, 'I clearly find you very, very attractive,' with such a frown on his face.

He thinks I'm better off on my own, I thought. What an ass. But he is trying to do the right thing, leaving the money for me to make it on my own, and all. I watched some more TV and waited some more.

As luck would have it, I wound up watching some old Clint Eastwood movie where he plays someone macho in the extreme. This lady's really hung up on him. He ends up screwing her and flying outta there, leaving a bundle of bills on her nightstand as he goes. Now that changed my perspective on the whole 'leaving me some cash to get by' thing. I was in no state to be confronted with a dose of Clint-sized chauvinism. Plus, the feeling I was conducting a stakeout was starting to wear thin. And I was hungry.

I left a note of my own, on the bed. It was kind of scrawly, too. Normally I have pretty good penmanship, but I was mad:

Dear Gunther,

Thanks for the wad of cash. Thanks for making me feel like a fucking whore.

I was too frustrated and hungry to formulate any further sentiments. And I thought that sufficed. (I don't have a problem with prostitutes per se, or most people who are judged harshly just for the sake of it, and Gunther knows that. But I think I demonstrated my point.) I went downstairs to the diner and ordered a tuna melt. I ordered a coffee, but then canceled it. It made me feel even more like I was on a stakeout. I got a chocolate milkshake instead. With my new windfall of cash.

Eating made me feel a little better. I even felt vaguely OK with my potential new-found independence. Although that was a tricky one, because I'd always thought choosing to drift around with Gunther *was* a matter of independent choice. My first choice; my premium existence. However, being by myself and feeling I could call the shots was slightly comforting.

The waitress was nice enough. She had long, straight, mousy hair, and had on jeans and a red sweater: pleasant looking. She had that comfortable attractiveness of people who don't try too hard, aren't trying to outshine you, but keep themselves up OK. The lack of uniform was disappointing, though. As tacky as they sometimes are, I like uniforms. I like how they make our roles more clearly defined. They make waitresses seem that much more like nurses. I like the feeling I'm being looked after. But uniform or no, she was very attentive, given I was so young and dining alone. But I didn't want her worrying and thinking I was *too* young. That sort of thing draws unwanted attention. I was liking my freedom. I left her a good tip and called her 'doll' on my way out.

By now it was completely dark out. I walked past the vending machine and thought about my vending-machine romances. They were little specks of nothing. I wish I could still be called upon to feel something for such basic things. Why can't I be moved anymore? Sometimes loving Gunther makes everything I see seem so happy and almost funny, like the whole world is a big sunny cartoon. When we're driving and I'm looking out at fields, horses, cows and crops, farmers, townspeople, other people in cars, I'm filled with the brightness of it all. Then there are times I can't give a damn for anything that isn't Gunther. It may as well be gray lumpy cold porridge. I don't care if it's people, or places, or time even.

The room was exactly as I left it, only darker. The thank-you note was there on the bed. Gunther's things were just as I left them. This was no real surprise. I caught myself in the mirror. I looked small and scared. And sad. I looked like a little rabbit in headlights. I switched on the TV. I watched something funny and didn't laugh. I rolled a joint. (Had he even packed spare underpants?) It occurred to me Gunther might be in trouble. It was weird how everything was still here. Except him. Something was wrong.

He's always been a weirdo, though. He moves in mysterious ways. And it's hard for me to judge these situations objectively, because, as I'm sure I've mentioned before, I find his absence very wrong, full stop.

I smoked my joint and channel surfed. I felt a little better. I'm not one of those people who wigs out on pot if they're feeling iffy. I guess I must associate it with the comforting rituals of Gunther and me. I was getting hazy and thought I could almost feel him again, out there, OK.

I watched a documentary on climate change. They'd assembled a group of experts who maintained that global warming was actually going to bring on an instant ice age. In our lifetime, probably. They bored down into the bottom of the ocean and brought up mud samples in chronological layers, like rings on a tree trunk. They could tell from the samples every time the Gulf Stream stopped flowing. Apparently when that happens there's an ice age, because the warm waters can't move warmth around the world. So places get cold and stay cold. And the Gulf Stream stops when there's not enough salt to sink down and force its current. As the earth warms up, the icebergs melt, filling the oceans with enough fresh water to thin out the salt until there's not enough of it to sink down and make the Gulf Stream flow.

I pictured Gunther and me sitting in a little

shack, with a fire blazing around us. That didn't seem so bad. I wondered if it would still be worth his turning me into a vampire and living together indefinitely in those harsh conditions. That seemed all right, still. Independence lost any and all of its positive qualities. There's no pride in spending an ice age by yourself. That was for Gunther and me. Huddling for warmth with Gunther. That's the only way to go. I think I pretty much do that anyway. I need him near when this ice age hits. Need to know where to find him.

I'm not mad this time. Just wondering how he can stand the tension of this distance between us. Why he doesn't just snap back to our closeness like a stretched rubber band. I ache for him to come back. But I know he won't, not as quickly as I feel he should. Because he feels things in his own way. And this is him. This is just something he does. Now that I started with all the touching. Maybe I *am* a whore. It seems wrong making someone recoil from you in torment. Someone you care for a lot. I knew he was weird about it, and I just kept it up.

I'm not religious by any means, but I said what was essentially a little prayer to Gunther as I drifted off to sleep. I tried to mind-meld with him out there on his Gunther trip. I told him I was done disrespecting his wishes, done pushing him too far, compromising his Gunther space and crossing his Gunther lines. If only he'd come back.

I woke the next morning with the first rays of the blinding sun, poking through the cracks of the dingy blinds. I wondered if today would bring Gunther. Somehow it didn't feel like it would. But, being a new day, it still carried the faint promise of Gunther.

I went into town and walked around. There weren't many people about. And 'town' consisted basically of one main street. There were a couple of diners, a gas station, a library. A knitting shop. I passed a couple of clothing stores that looked like they hadn't changed their window displays since the 1950s. The mannequins were dusty, and looked even more tortured than usual. Never mind about the clothes.

I had breakfast at one of the diners; eggs on white toast, bottomless coffee. I deliberated on pancakes, but wasn't happy enough. Nor was I feeling sorry enough for myself to warrant cheering up via comfort food. I had what I deemed a man's breakfast, minus the bacon (too salty, and pigs are just so damn loveable). Then I went and sat in the library.

I found a book on Egon Schiele, sat at a table and looked at the pictures. Egon is Gunther's favourite artist. He took me to an exhibition of Austrian expressionists on one of the rare occasions we stopped in a city. He's pretty good at locating retro movie theatres, too. He likes to try and get us a cultural fix every now and then. We once found an arthouse cinema in a town so tiny all it seemed to have in it was this cinema. We saw Betty Blue. Now there's a chick who latched onto a man and was truly crazy. I'm not that out there. Besides, I didn't feel like I was latching on until after the fact. Seems to me like I was invited.

I sat there and read about the life of Egon Schiele. He and his wife both got sick and died young. His artwork must have been pretty shocking for his day, because it's semi-pornographic by today's standards, but then, what a fucking bunch of prudes everyone is today. I don't think Egon would have cared either way. In his words (written in calligraphy on the inner sleeve of the book), 'Art cannot be modern; art is eternal'.

I find Egon Schiele's paintings to be a touch haughty. I can see why Gunther likes him. But out of all those old expressionists, I like Richard Gerstl, who committed suicide young and left barely any work behind to show for it. Gunther says I have highly advanced tastes. But it's pointless to write about art when it's not there for people to see.

Checking the motel again for signs of Gunther was a compulsion I tried to but could not resist. I meandered a little, but there was no point in kidding myself, I really wanted to just make a bee line for the room, so that's what I ended up doing.

He was sitting up in bed with his ankles crossed, smoking a joint. He hadn't even bothered to take off his shoes. But then, in a dump like this, who cares?

'Have a good time?' he droned, evenly. Goddamn the King of Cool. I just looked at him.

'Spend all the money?' Just as cas.

'No,' I stammered. 'Some of it. I had eggs.' I shrugged. 'And stuff.'

He smiled graciously. I knew he could tell I was upset. And it seemed like such a weakness, all this raw emotion of mine. He beamed down on me from that filthy rooms-by-the-hour motel bed, looking like someone had stretched a Buddha. All long and thin, exuding calmness, kindness.

He handed me the joint, in a slow fluid

movement. I took it, and flopped down on the bed next to him. We both stared straight ahead in silence. God knows what he was thinking; I was wondering where the fuck he'd been these past few days. He couldn't possibly have dames everywhere. Besides, I don't think Gunther's libido's all it used to be. He keeps to himself, and I coax him out.

After we'd passed the joint back and forth and I'd had several good tokes, it struck me how perfectly the vampire scenario explained the unexplainable absences. If I had to duck out and slaughter some semi-innocent victims for the purpose of sucking their blood, I wouldn't tell my loved ones, either.

We switched the TV on and watched the news. Some little girl had gone missing in the next town over. And the next county had been swept by a tornado. There was an autoworkers' strike, and they were predicting a drought.

Gunther said, 'Hungry?'

I said, 'Yeah.'

Damn it how Gunther seemed to know his way around every town, no matter what a back-water it was, and how much he seemed like a piece of velvet on a hessian sack. Like a cat padding through his territory, he drove us to a well-decent little restaurant off the beaten track.

Hell, was it romantic. There were candles and red wine. No one seemed to care that I was way underage. I just sat across from him beaming. He returned my gaze with plenty of feeling, and that touch of kindly pity that seemed to be increasing as the evening wore on; seemed to be increasing in direct proportion to the rise in my romantic zeal. After all, it was nearly bedtime.

In the car, on the way home—on the way back to the sleazy motel—I told him about the ice age.

I explained the whole thing, with as much scientific accuracy as I could. I covered the mud samples, the Gulf Stream, the sinking salt, the melting ice caps, the increased global warming, et cetera.

He grinned sadly, with no hint of teeth, and said, 'Is that what we have in store for us?'

I said, 'Yes, it is!' and involuntarily leaned in toward him. I desperately want to share that phase of existence with him, bound together by love and necessity, watching this mad planet get its own back. That was definitely in store for us. He must understand that. There would be no disappearing for several days, driving off without a clue. He *could* do that, but he would lose all his warmth, all his shelter and safety; all that would undoubtedly become sacred.

When we got back to the motel, and I stretched out my arms toward him, he said, 'I'm sorry. I can't do this anymore.' He drew back a half step. 'I never meant to.'

Again, I only stared.

'I'm old…er than you,' he said, by way of feeble explanation. 'You know? You're not old enough to even know what you want. I can't take someone like that.'

'And you're old enough to not want anything anymore,' I snapped.

'I want things.' He sounded genuinely hurt. I didn't anticipate such flippancy could have an impact on Sir. Master of His Own Domain. Mr. Even Keel.

'I want you to know my sincerest friendship. As I do for all my dear…special friends.'

Oh Gunther, ever the disarming one. Hearing him call me 'dear' and 'special' quieted me down. But I was still feeling princessy enough to fuss over the point of having to share him with the rest of these gourmet friends, and wondered how many we were talking. I'll always want to be his special #1, the way he is for me.

'Friends are a very special thing,' he said.

I said, 'I know.'

I crawled into the fetal position on one side of the bed and tried to sleep. I tossed off clothes intermittently, and strewed them on the floor. I wasn't sure how much to take off, now that the line had been drawn at 'just friends' again. But I wanted to be comfy.

He turned the lights off and tried to sleep, too. It seemed so unnatural, forcing ourselves to stay apart like that. It was hard to sleep with the tension of it. He must have felt the energy coming off me the way, I was sure, I felt the energy coming off him, because by morning I was wrapped in his arms. We didn't get up to anything. Just held each other.

He got up even earlier than usual, and started on his morning routine. I could tell we were leaving by the nature of his preparations. Everything was going back in its place. Things were finding their way into orderly piles. I was still lying in bed, watching him.

He came and sat on the edge of the bed. He had on a button-down shirt, his undies, and socks. Gunther never was too concerned about covering up and all that. Let's face it; we've been sharing hotel rooms for a while now. And we're practically family. Better than family.

He said, 'I don't want to hurt you anymore.'

'OK.'

'I was happier being your humble chauffeur.'

We piled everything into the car, and when I slid in beside him, he said, 'Where to, Miss?'

I vaguely remembered my days as a frustrated small-town bumpkin, dreaming of a promising and colorful existence in the big smoke. Besides, I thought we'd already decided.

'New York City?'

'New York City.'

The words filled me with sort of a sick euphoria. I was destined to have an interesting life after all. What's more, Gunther did love me, but from the abstracted distance of just wanting me to be me. The optimal me, that is. Fulfilling potential and all that. Just following him around like a puppy dog probably isn't the best I can do with myself. I guess. I don't like pining after him in his absences, that's for sure.

It's a long, hot drive to wherever Gunther has us headed next, and I've had plenty of time to think. I thought, I wouldn't be looking like a silly puppy if he loved me properly back. Everything would be OK.

He'll probably be dropping me in NYC permanently, after these little trial runs of leaving me stuck in the middle of fucking nowhere for a few days. At least there will be stuff for me to get on with in a proper city. But the thought of him leaving forever is...unthinkable. Surely that could not be his intention, after all this time out here bonding, getting to know each other out here on the road. Unless he considers himself some kind of Buddha master, instructing me until he decides I'm ready to tackle the world alone. Sometimes it feels that way.

Vampires don't do that, though. They don't go to all that trouble with someone and just desert them. You live that long, you see how fucked up the world is, you travel around...you find a friend, you stick to them. You find someone to love, you make them your obedient slave. You bind them to you by sheer need. A loneliness that immense needs to be shared.

I shot him a look. Me and my overactive imagination! But looking at him there didn't help matters. He was squinting palely into the sun, looking withered but dashing. Looking every bit like he'd like nothing more than to climb back into his coffin, wrap himself in the satin lining.

We stopped for lunch at a pizza parlor. I was

pretty sure Gunther made eyes at the waitress. She wasn't even pretty. She was kind of nervous. The food was average. I got a calzone, which was spelled 'callzoni' on the menu. I couldn't get out of there fast enough. Gunther was being way too nice to that dame.

Maybe he was just trying to spread himself around again. I'm feeling a little the same way. In a way it's been nice to stop all that romantic crap; all that touching. I don't have to worry about what I'm doing wrong, and if it's going to make him go away again. He doesn't have to act so guilty around me. Things are almost back to normal.

We hung around town for a while. The streets were covered with red dust. I sat down by the car and painted bottle caps. Gunther kept a bag of paints in the glove box. He's a much better artist than me. He came back from his walk and said, 'Oh, look at you, with your folk art!'

Damn Gunther has a name for everything.

Then he said, 'Little bottle cap miniatures!'

I smiled up at him.

'May I have one?'

I gave him a little happy skull with a bone in its mouth. He cradled it in his palm, and carried it back to the car. We got back on the road and tried to get as far as we could before dark. I rolled a joint. I smoked and watched the land stretch out all around us.

It looked just the same. The world, that is. The road; the shimmering gray asphalt, pea-green grass, people's houses, people's barns, people's cars, the trees, were all unmoved and unchanged by recent events. Gunther and I, an item…Gunther and I, just friends. Me, precocious slut, tempting Gunther to nail me. Me, repentant youngster trying like hell to learn some respect for my elder(s) again. The sun just ruthlessly shines.

'Gunther,' I said, 'the sun is so relentless.'

I leaned over and handed him the joint. It wasn't official Gunther Smoking Time. But he grinned a faint grin and took it. He smoked it a damn long time (Bogarting if you ask me) then handed it back in slow motion. Zen and the art of handing over a joint. I think it took a full thirty seconds for it to reach my hand. And it looked like he was flying it in on a little plane. I was deeply amused.

'Gunther,' I said, 'you're not getting this back.'

He laughed heartily. 'Well, I *am* driving.'

'Yes, you are.'

Apparently this was funny, too.

The town we reached as the sun was setting looked to consist of little more than a whorehouse and a gas station. Men were actually having fisticuffs by the side of the road. We drove straight through. Gunther asked me if I'd like us to drive another hour and a half or so to a bigger town he knew was half decent. I said yes.

We had a big pasta dinner, found a movie house, and watched Citizen Kane. I was too stoned to remember much about it, apart from the fact that it was long, and that an old man liked his sled.

I was so tired when we got back to the room, I flopped down on the bed, kicked my shoes off, and said, 'Goodnight, Gunther.' I hadn't even brushed my teeth.

'Goodnight,' he said, with no shortage of tenderness. He was sitting in an armchair.

When I awoke the next morning he was already running the taps. He must have been halfway through his morning procedure. I was worried things would be weird now. Staying perpetually wasted was clearly the key to weaning myself off the carnal side of our dealings with no trace of awkwardness. I can be warm and sleepy, and just glad he's there.

We had breakfast to go at a really nice old-style bakery. I got a blueberry muffin. Gunther got a ham and cheese croissant. Then more driving, driving, driving. I didn't roll a joint this time. I was kind of groggy.

Seems like we've been on the road half of forever. We stopped at a crappy roadside diner sometime in the afternoon. I swear Gunther flirted with that waitress, too. And she was not much to look at either. Permed yellow hair, cigarette hangin' out of the side of her mouth. Isn't that a health violation? She may as well have had 'NOT GUNTHER'S TYPE' tattooed across her forehead. I picked at my meal and moved it in piles around my plate, muttering things like, 'Is that mashed potato gray?'

Was Gunther always this charming? I don't seem to recall. I remember him being happy in my presence. I recall feeling like co-conspirators in something I didn't fully understand, but was stoked to be a part of.

So more closeness has yielded more distance. And the earth getting hotter will bring about an ice age. My head hurts. And I must be getting old now. Because it seems I'm starting to make crucial errors, rack up regrets, and muddle around in them. Sitting here smoking, looking at Gunther, typing on the typewriter. It hurts now.

He's still physically exactly the same. That Gunther sitting there, watching the news, in those slacks, in his brown shirt, with his elegance and his moody calm. That's the same Gunther from the happy innocent cocoon days. The same Gunther of limitless passion, horizonless love. And so am I: the same. Those are my scrawny bitten chipped black nails on the keys. My mousy hair falling over my eyes.

A morning shower bright and early confirmed this further. I wiped the steam from the mirror. That's me; it was always there, that little blank mouse face staring accusingly back at me.

'You're up early,' said Gunther.

'Yeah,' I said, and mumbled, 'Like two ships passing in the morning.'

'Hmmm?'

'Nothing.' I am really not a morning person, and I probably should never attempt to get up before him.

I found a video channel and blared loud music while Gunther took his shower.

A song came on that knocked me for six. Now, I know it's cheese, but sometimes cheese hits you the hardest. A pretty-boy loud band. They said:

I just lost my best friend. I miss you so much I wish my life would end…(something, something) *And I can't let go. Because it hurts like I've never been hurt before…I cannot sleep without you here. All I wanted was to be with you* (something…)

Or something like that.

Gunther came out wrapped in a towel and made some disparaging comments about the lead singer's haircut. He didn't see my eyes welling with tears. My wet hair was falling over my face, dripping onto my lap.

It was an overcast day, one of those silvery-gray ones. I slouched in the passenger seat, staring out at the sky's metallic glare. I couldn't tell if I was quietly weeping all day, or if my eyes were just sensitive. I'm generally not a crier.

We drove all day and ate nothing but corn chips. We had a bag stashed on the back seat.

Gunther's in the shower. I get the impression he's going out. Just a hunch. I'm not getting the social vibe. We've barely spoken all day. I wouldn't say it was an uncomfortable silence, it's more like we're just tired.

Now he's trudged back into the room with his lank wet hair and asked if I'm hungry. I said not really. Sometimes sitting in the car all day makes you feel like a slug. He said, 'Yeah. I'm not either. I have kind of a headache. I think I'll go for a walk.'

Jeez, I hope that's not a euphemism for anything. I feel like stealing his car keys. But I also feel kind of numb about it all now.

So, as it were, Gunther went out, and I stayed in and got as stoned as possible. I watched little snippets of various crappy TV shows. I daydreamed. I missed having Gunther around to talk stoned shit with; missed him, full stop. He was a solid entity. Being stoned without him was just too floaty. I never know where the hell I am. I fell asleep. I heard Gunther come in much later. He was fumbling around with his keys. He must have been drunk, which is an exceedingly rare occurrence. Almost enough of a curiosity to warrant turning on the lights and attempting a chat. Drunk Gunther is one Gunther I am relatively unfamiliar with. He smelled funny. He crashed onto the bed like a felled redwood. God, why is he being such an anti-hero?

This room had two double beds, and we had one each. We must have woken up around the same time. The first thing I saw the next morning was Gunther lying motionless on his side, gaping bloodshot eyes pointing straight at me. He looked like a corpse. I felt the corners of my mouth turning up tenderly. (Gunther calls this my cat smile. He says cross the Mona Lisa with the empathy of the all-knowing housecat, and you have my smile.) More of a faint grin, really. I suppose Gunther and I are alike in that respect.

He said, 'Good morning, sunshine.'

I said, 'Morning.'

'Might sleep a while longer,' he said, then craned his neck toward the digital alarm clock and moaned, 'Ach, I already have.'

There was no point in missing checkout time. Clearly Gunther had already had all the fun there was to have in this town.

I had another few hours in the passenger seat, of just staring out the window. I figure we must be getting near our destination now. America's funny that way. You'll feel like you're in the middle of the most forsaken dreamless expanse of nowhere, a crater. Then you get a half an hour of strip malls, then half an hour of 'burbs and crappy townships. Then you're in some fucking huge city. All of a sudden it rises up, like Godzilla out of the ocean. This huge factory, spewing people and money, glitz and garbage, noise, smoke, and so many promises.

Unfortunately I am only aware of one promise at this stage. The only thing I can be nearly certain of is that there will be no me and Gunther there. I can stop wondering if and where he is going to drop me. He is dropping me there.

We're not zig-zagging around the country anymore. Not visiting friends.

'Gunther?'

'Hmmm?' He shoots me a sideways glance. He is concentrating very hard on the task of operating a vehicle today. He looks even more pallid, if that were possible. Glowing, borderline light blue.

'We never visit friends anymore. You never take me to visit friends.' I noticed the visits stopped pretty much around the time I jumped him, and the shame started to set in. He was ashamed of me. Maybe all he was doing during his disappearances was visiting friends on his own. He didn't like what he was doing with me, and could only feel like himself again without me. Or maybe he was trying to prove he didn't feel a thing for me, by porking his way around the country. I can't really imagine it; can't really see Gunther gathering the compulsion to be intimate with that many ladies in so short a time. He's given me several indications that he is not as motivated by lusty pursuits as he used to be. He said he just didn't feel like it anymore. But then, he has always been the secretive one.

'Well, we can if you want to,' he replied, casually, and then mumbled to himself, 'Hair of the dog.'

We stopped for lunch at a kind of truck stop diner. Gunther ordered a doughnut. It must be a cold day in hell. I've started bringing the typewriter into places with me, and I've got it here. It's light, and I can just put it up on the table, and write about Gunther while he's sitting there. I like lining up new blank pages, winding them into position. It makes me feel like I have something important to tell. We're talking less lately; I may as well. He doesn't seem to mind much. I know he minds a little, because he sits there grimacing at me, but there's a hint of a smile there, too.

'Why don't you ever write?' I asked him. 'Or draw?' By this stage I was doodling on a napkin. I've seen Gunther's handiwork before. The first time I decided he was truly a vampire, and didn't just look like one, was standing in front of his painting of old Glorie. It would take more than a lifetime to amass that much skill and talent, I decided. And then I found out he could play the harp. The fucking *harp*. Do mortals play that?

'You're young,' he said. 'So young,' and all the old tenderness flooded back into his face. 'You have a lot to express.'

The waitress came over and started fussing over my napkin sketch. I'd done a drawing of the resident dog, who was curled up by the register. I said she could have it. She was positively swooning. I don't think they get many interesting visitors through here. Or health inspectors.

She wandered off waving the picture at the dog, saying, 'Oh, Pinchy, look! It's you!' Mostly I just draw to pass the time. I usually leave them behind; after all, they are napkins. So it wasn't a big deal, giving her that one.

Not going to bother describing her. Stock standard waitress. Gunther hasn't appeared to flirt with her. Maybe he's over that phase. Or maybe he's just too ill. God, he did order a doughnut. And ate it, no less.

I took another napkin out of the dispenser and drew a cartoon of Gunther's stomach barring a doughnut's admission. It was basically just a coil of intestines, with a speech bubble saying, 'I'm sorry, you have the wrong stomach.'

'Jeez, Gunther, I'm surprised your stomach doesn't have a Do Not Enter sign for food like that.'

He grinned.

'You're such a fussy little eater.' I giggled.

I'd gone back to the typewriter by now. Gunther picked the tummy cartoon out of a little pile.

'May I?' he asked.

'Yeah, 'course,' I said. He folded it into his breast pocket.

No one wants me. They only want the *little* pieces.

When we hit the road again Gunther headed off in an entirely different direction. We had been going east. We were now going south. Southwest, if anything. Within two hours, we were pulling up to a shack, situated in the middle of an expanse of barren grasslands. It looked like a military testing site. Barely fit for human habitation. But then, it seemed to suit the inhabitant. And there is something strangely calming about environments that sparse.

And something clearly maddening…

Her name's Delilah. She has dozens of wind chimes hanging from the roof of her seriously basic wooden cabin, encasing the front porch. I can't imagine them ever chiming here. The wind doesn't seem to ever blow. The sound of flies buzzing is the most prominent sound out here. The occasional plane flies overhead. And jets, too, to complete the military outpost feel. It is dreamily fucking boring here. After one glass of her Kentucky bourbon I felt like running around the porch yelling and smacking wind chimes, like a hyperactive three-year-old banging pots and pans. Environments that calm are anything but, in my book. Gunther says I have an active brain that requires stimulus.

Delilah was as drunk as a sailor's whore when we got here, and insisted we reach the same state, A.S.A.P. She fixed Gunther up with a bourbon on the rocks, and when she pushed one on me, I glanced at Gunther. He gave me a pointed but reassuring 'where are your manners' nod. I guess this was one of those 'when in Rome' situations. Alcohol is probably Gunther's least favorite intoxicant. He considers it poison, and generally doesn't encourage me to partake in it. But that doesn't stop him, on occasion.

Delilah was damn glad to see Gunther, but she was also so drunk the impact of the occasion seemed lost on her. She was acting like he just wandered over from next door or something. Like she saw him every day. But liked him a lot nonetheless. Thought he was a good sort.

'So, little kitten,' she slumped toward me. She was seated in a big wicker extravaganza. She gripped the arm of my rocking chair. I had to brace my feet on the floor to keep from toppling backward. 'Gunther usually travels alone.'

That hung in the air for a while. Then I said, 'Yeah, well, he's giving me a ride.'

'Tha's nice,' she slurred. About thirty seconds later she blurted joyfully, 'I'll bet he is!'

Gunther and I both looked at her in reproachful silence.

She retreated with, 'Naw, no. Gunther's a perfect gentleman.' She paused another thirty seconds or so and exclaimed, 'Nowadays! Ah, Gunther!' She winked, lurched over and slapped him on the arm as she said this. There was another reproachful (but bemused) silence from Gunther and me.

She retracted this statement, too. 'No, no, you were always the gentleman…Gunther, Gunther, Gunther.'

Now let me describe her. Lots of jangly jewelry, and wild fluffy hennaed hair. Borderline chubby. She has on overalls, with daisy buttons. She looks like someone inflated a toddler. But then her face, under all those browny-red curls, is weathered and creased. There's a black and white photo of her inside, from her flower child hey-day. She looks like a million bucks.

She tottered into the kitchen and started clanging pots around. She was making a pretty good stab at cooking us a big pasta dinner, given her state. Gunther and I gave her a hand. The resulting meal was a modestly good group effort. I was so damn hungry anyway, a hearty pasta went down a treat. Those two had red wine with theirs. Despite drinking hers with rapidity, Delilah appeared to sober up a tad during the course of the meal.

Turns out she's a writer. A journalist, no less. Has assignments here, there, and everywhere. Manages to make a decent living out of freelance stuff. I can't imagine her overheads being very high, living out here on the plateau…She'd been out to Chicago to interview homeless people. Then over to the neighboring county, to cover the trapping of a puma.

She had another crack at the subject of Gunther

and me toward the tail end of dinner. We weren't giving anything away. She asked if I had a boyfriend anywhere, and I said no. She asked me a few more questions in this vein, which I answered gruffly and noncommittally. I guess my moody indifference toward the subject of all things romantic spurred her on even more, because she leaned over my plate and said, 'Sweet stuff?'

'Yeah?' I ventured.

'If I looked like you, I'd be giving it to everyone!' She threw her head back and cackled joyously. She righted her head, and took a healthy swig of wine.

It was earlier than it seemed. The sun was still up. I was tired, but we headed into town. Delilah was insistent we experience the local nightlife, which was in surprisingly close proximity to her large patch of dirt and sparse grasses.

There was a crazy energy to this puny town. A few dozen drunken paces from Delilah's, and we were in the thick of it. Main Street was bright and positively raucous. It was the old boredom + alcohol combo. These people knew how to whoop it up.

Gunther said, 'Jack lives here, all right.'

We always laugh at those goddamn try-hard ads.

Delilah said, 'You got that right, hot lips.'

That started a wave of giggles.

'Gunther!' I said, 'did you roll us a joint?'

'Why yes I did, sweet buns,' he drawled.

I was laughing proper by now.

Delilah said, 'I *knew* you guys had something.'

Gunther fired up the joint and handed it to me as we strolled along.

'Hey, put that thing out!' Delilah belted. 'You wanna get the sheriff's department down on us?'

'Cops?' Gunther sounded amused. 'Here? So… public drinking, fornicating, and maiming, all OK, just don't try and smoke here. Is that what you're saying?'

'Yes, that is what I'm saying.'

I put the joint out on my belt buckle. I handed it to Gunther, who put it back in his tin.

'Thanks, honey tits.'

'Shut *up!*' I snapped.

Delilah muttered, 'Knew it all along.'

We walked three abreast through the wide entrance of a crowded bar, which was noisy of course. It seemed somehow quieter than it was out on the street. Maybe it was the music (Guns N' Roses), acting as white noise. Underage drinking seemed to be the norm here. I saw an androgynous kid who looked about twelve slumped on the step, cradling a beer. I did what any teenager worth a dime would do: fronted up to the bar and ordered myself a drink.

Delilah and Gunther were down the bar a little ways. I was savoring my independence, probably more than my beer, which tasted kind of bitter. An affable redneck appeared at the bar beside me and ordered himself the same swill I was drinking. They had it on tap there. He looked youngish, with dark red hair and big fuzzy flaming sideburns.

He asked me where I'm from, and a few other small-talky questions. He seemed genuinely curious. I don't think he was trying to score or anything. He nodded to those two down the bar, and asked if I was with them. I said, 'yeah'. He said he thought he saw us come in together.

Then he gave a curt nod in Gunther's direction and said, 'That guy looks at you with fuckin' love in his face, man.'

I said, 'We're just friends.'

'Just friends?' he snorted. 'Not likely.'

'Go ahead and ask him. He's not into anything with me.'

He snorted again. 'That's the oldest trick in the

book, missy. Treat 'em mean, keep 'em keen.'

I pondered this. I've always found that saying idiotic. He added, 'You chicks dig a challenge.' His goofy smirk was widening between those huge sideburns. 'I'm telling you: love in his face.'

I looked over at Gunther. He wasn't looking at me. He was talking to Delilah. It did seem like a long shot, but then I guess you believe what you want to believe. I shouldn't have, maybe, but I gave the Treat 'em Mean Theory my full consideration. It gained more plausibility as the night wore on. Each beer added more weight to the subject, like little devils lining up on my shoulder, whispering in my ear, telling me it all made sense now.

The jukebox cranked out a steady stream of loud, hard numbers. Not a single song you couldn't dance to. I danced with girls, I danced with guys. Mostly I just danced by myself, with my eyes half-closed, in a little corner of the dance floor. Someone put on 'Venus'. I like that song. It's an oldie but a goodie. I glanced across at Gunther. For a second I thought I could see what Sideburns was talking about. It was one of those nights when I like being pretty, I like being alive.

We stumbled back out onto the street several

hours later. There were only a few stragglers out now. You could hear the rural silence; feel its presence. We were laughing at I don't know what. Just laughing for the sake of laughing at this stage, I think. Gunther was in such good spirits I really felt I had nothing to lose.

Delilah snagged herself on the door beads on her way back into the shack. She'd left the front door open, but I reckon in this town, door beads make for pretty good security. A struggle ensued that sent several strands flying, scattering beads everywhere. And Gunther's and my attempts to free her nearly ensnared us both. She flailed around like an octopus caught in seaweed for a while, then finally broke free with one grand finale of a bead cascade.

Three drunks attempting to traverse a room with a floor covered in slippery beads turned into quite a spectacle. Gunther made it across OK, eventually. He has longer legs than us, so didn't have to risk as many teetering steps. Once he was on solid ground, he reached across to me. I fell on my ass in the first attempt to reach his hand. When I was at last dragged to safety we turned to Delilah, who was crawling on all fours. That proved effective; she made it across the last few feet relatively speedily, unassisted.

We regrouped by the couch. Delilah said, 'Well, I'm gonna hit the hay.' Do people talk that way *just* because they live in the country? 'Gunther, you can take the couch, and you'—nodding at me—'can have the guest bed.' There was a cot set up in a room next to hers, the size of a closet. Then she added, chortling, 'Unless you two lovebirds want to sleep together…'

She clumped heavily down the hall, slammed her door and, by the sound of things, collapsed onto the bed.

I turned to Gunther gleefully, grabbed his hand and spouted, 'Why not?'

A mix of emotion danced briefly across his face. Then it was gone, and he said somberly, 'Didn't I make myself clear?'

'Yes you did.'

He gingerly handed me my hand back.

I fell into my cot and passed out pretty much straight away. I woke up to find I'd dribbled vomit on myself and onto the pillow. I crept out of my room and gave my shirt and the pillowcase a good scrubbing in the bathroom sink. I wadded them up with the intention of hanging them in my room, and scurried back down the hall. I didn't want Delilah to catch me; I wasn't up for the wisecracks she'd deliver. There wasn't much chance anyway; I could hear her snoring in her room. And I was in no mood to face Gunther, even though I could be sure he would be ingratiatingly helpful in regard to the task at hand.

Those two finally woke up, and Delilah and I sat on the front porch while she smoked a cigarette. Gunther was in the shower. I asked her if she truly thought Gunther and I were an item.

'Heck no, kiddo!' she burst forth, good-naturedly. 'I'm just cranking his shaft. Well, mostly.'

She took a pointed drag on her cigarette and added, 'Old Gunther's about the only guy alive who could travel around with a pretty little thing like you and not try anything on.'

'Hmmm.' I meant this to sound contemplative, not dejected, and I'm quite sure I failed.

'Nowadays...he's like one of those Buddhist monks who tries not to step on anything...bugs. Doesn't like to stir a thing. Good old Gunther.'

I thought about this. As it happened, an ant was making its way across the porch, inching along, toward my legs. Saving this ant from being crushed under someone's big foot does seem like an act of mercy. Steadfastly refusing to return someone's love for you; I just can't see the mercy in that. Surrendering to the force of our unquenchable feelings seems more graceful, humbly respectful to the will of the universe.

But I'm reasonably certain Gunther doesn't see it that way. I guess Gunther has done a lot of touching in his time, and now he doesn't want to touch anything else. Or anything else to touch him.

I said 'Hmmm' again to Delilah. She puffed a puff of smoke at me, cast a smile in my direction.

Gunther came and sat down on my other side. Delilah started singing 'Blue Velvet'.

I muttered, 'Sorry about last night,' with a touch of sarcasm Gunther failed to detect.

He said, 'No need to apologize! We were all so drunk.'

'...Yeah.'

'What's that, Chookums?' Delilah gave me another look of amusement as she struggled to her feet and ambled down the hall toward the kitchen. We followed suit.

I said, 'I don't think I've heard that one before.'

'No, you wouldn't have. I think you'll find I'm very inventful.' Then she added, 'Gotta do something to pass the time around here.'

'Wouldn't get that one past your editor, would you?' asked Gunther.

'You'd be surprised.'

We ate fried eggs and ham. Then Gunther and I said thanks, bye, and headed off. We didn't drive very far that day. In fact, we only drove a half day. I think Gunther was pretty hungover. He checked us into a hotel and ran a bath in what was, by his standards, a very unhygienic bathtub. I sat on the bed and watched TV, one of those chair-smashing, shit-yelling talk shows.

Now, all those finger-pointing loonies that go on those shows are all the same. They all want love and approval from the very same people they're leveling flaming accusations at, the same people they're calling evil. Although maybe they're only evil because they can't love these finger-pointers.

A lady in the audience was saying, 'Usually when a man says he doesn't know what he wants, he doesn't know *who* he wants.'

This got my head spinning in ways I don't need it to. I have enough pressing concerns. Now it's got me pondering the unexplained absences all over again. Jeez, was Gunther out there doing the

Potential Female Sampler? Have I been a damn fool all this time? That would certainly account for all his hesitation and mixed emotion. His failure to commit to me, to us. Why the hell should I be competing with nothing? And coming out second best, I might add. I must be competing with something.

Gunther came out and sprawled on the bed to take a nap. It was no good watching him lie there with no chance of curling up next to him. I had to get out of there.

I gravitated to the center of town, and wandered the streets looking at all the people. Seemed like a lot of people looked vaguely lonely. It certainly wasn't just me. I passed a dorky-looking guy with a glassy stare and big headphones on. He'd certainly pre-prepared himself for a solitary walk.

As I walked, and passed all those other bodies, it didn't seem to matter if I lived or died. I cursed the day Cupid, that fat little fuck, that aimless archer, shot me. (God, I've always hated cherubs.) Shot me through the heart and made me love Gunther, the jaded nomadic hermit, instead of all the other guys who look at me with lust in their eyes and bouquets in their hearts.

I've been opened. I'm out here in the world,

like a lidless jar, filling with urges and desire. I don't know where to put it all. It courses through me. I need someone now. I need anyone. It doesn't matter anymore. He doesn't love me like I love him.

Now there was this guy walking toward me who looked like Benicio del Toro circa Fear and Loathing, in a sweaty tank top. I felt like pushing this fella to the ground and riding him bucking bronco style.

Darkness fell, and I propeled myself through the doors of a bar. I was settled on a stool in an instant, tapping the Formica impatiently.

The bartender eyed me over. 'Bit young, aren't you?'

'Yeah, but I bet you like 'em that way,' I said dryly.

He snorted out a single laugh and raised his eyebrows at me expectantly.

'Whiskey and Coke,' I said.

He said, 'On the house.' And poured about three shots of whiskey into my glass. 'Probably watered down, anyway,' I thought.

There were a few guys around. And they weren't ignoring me. When I finished my drink and made to order another, there was quite a competition as to who was going to get me my next one. I've always found it funny guys think this signifies something. To us girls it mostly just signifies a free drink, as far as I know. But then, there are those who say nothing comes free.

I downed one after the other of these free drinks. The guys just kept them coming. And there was laughter all 'round. But I wouldn't say I was in good spirits. I found myself sitting in this circle of leering admirers, wishing Gunther had turned me into a vampire, like I'd fantasized all those times. I wished I could lure them into an alley somewhere and turn them into my unwitting feast. Wished I could spend my nights in these towns biting the boys, then going back and wrapping myself in Gunther's arms (and maybe something velvet).

It came up to closing time, and we got kicked out onto the street. There was a bit of discussion about what I was doing now, and with whom. I said I should probably get going back to the hotel. Two guys won the privilege of walking me. Two guys seemed safe enough. They were both average looking, normally dressed, middle-of-the-road types. Some women probably would have found them good looking, but there's me: I have odd tastes, and I can only carry one torch at a time. Hell knows that torch for Gunther burns pretty bright…I thought about him back there at the hotel, and knew coming home to him would be a mixed blessing. I am always too glad to see him.

These two were jostling for dibs on me the whole time we walked. Then I got an idea.

I said, 'No need to fight over me.'

They both looked at me like all their Christmases had come at once. We headed across a parking lot, through a field and over to some old sheds. Those guys both started unzipping—talk about a hurry; Gunther always likes to take his time. The one in the plaid shirt grabbed my head and started kissing me. The other, in the football jersey, just watched for now. It had occurred to me that having the attention of two guys might be kind of thrilling, sort of gratifying.

They both started fumbling with my clothes. Plaid got my shirt off and started squishing my breasts around. Football dropped his pants to his ankles, and did the same to me, undies and all. Before I knew it, Plaid was inside me, pumping away. I hadn't considered which orifices they planned on utilizing. I figured they'd just take turns. God, I am such a baby. Football grabbed me from behind, and started poking around back there. In the spirit of the moment, I just let him. I'm not one to shy away from trying new things. Then I felt the searing pain. I tried not to moan. And then I tried not to scream. It hurt so much I felt like I was losing consciousness. I heard myself screaming. Someone clapped a hand over my mouth. It didn't seem like the pain would ever stop. The hand left my mouth and was replaced by a penis. They let go of me. I heard zippers, footsteps, then slid to the ground and just lay there.

I'd read about this girl in Australia. She was raped and left to die in a farmer's field. The farmer had driven out in the morning, and noticed his cows standing in an inward-facing circle. When he got home that evening, they were still standing there, staring at something. He got out of the car and walked over to see what they'd been looking at all day. It was the body of the girl.

That was nearly how I felt; how broken my body felt. I felt I should be lying in a circle of cows. But I wasn't. I was just sitting there dully on the asphalt. Everything burned. I was sure I was bleeding. And this was all my fucking fault.

I closed my eyes. I opened them to a loud wailing. The sun was up. There was a small crowd around me. I was being loaded into an ambulance.

People drifted in and out of my hospital room, asking me what had happened, and/or poking at various sore bits. I kept saying nothing, just a drunken orgy with two guys. Most of them said it didn't look like a party to them. None of them were Gunther. They were no good to me. Then finally he came.

He looked positively haunted. He collapsed into the bedside chair. He'd obviously been briefed, because he was hell-bent on delivering these guys to justice.

'No, Gunther. Gunther, it was my idea,' I cried.

'No it…' He grimaced. 'No it wasn't.'

'I thought it would be an interesting experience. You've done all that sort of thing…lots of people.'

He looked utterly aghast. 'You don't have to try to impress me.'

I thought of the art galleries, the reading, the mind-expanding drugs and deep conversations, and said, a touch brightly for the circumstances, 'But impressing you is making me a better person.'

He just stared.

I added, 'A more…learned person.'

'Oh god.' He threw his arms around me and held

me, much the same way he had Stephanie, when she woefully tried to seduce him.

Jeez, I never wanted his pity.

I was in hospital a few days. Gunther's calls for blood went nowhere. It turns out one of them, I don't even know which, was the police chief's son. Half the town was calling me a whore, and I wasn't doing much to defend myself. Gunther said they had no right to hurt me, to take advantage of me like that. I kept telling him it was my idea. He kept telling me it wasn't.

On the third night they put a junkie in the bed next to mine. It was pleasant when it was just the two of us in our room. His name was Elliot. We were having all kinds of dreamy conversations. He asked me if I was on morphine. I said yeah, I thought I was. I said I'd always had a feeling I'd like opiates.

Gunther's tried every kind of drug there is to try. I've always been partial to the notion of trying heroin, because I've always gotten along like a house on fire with junkies. I like that day-dreamy state. Gunther told me not to try that one. So did Elliot, now.

But even as he said that, I felt the lure of its warmth and protection. I could see he was wrapped in bliss. And I liked talking to him, liked his gentle calm. We talked about a lot of things. We spent a long, lingering while hovering on every subject, like two pixies jumping from cloud to cloud.

I told him about the artist, Egon Schiele, saying art is eternal. I asked him if he thought love was like that. Because what's acceptable and what's not changes throughout the ages. Hell, people used to get married at twelve. And do anything with anyone. It wasn't always love, but some of it was. We tried it out: 'Love cannot be modern: love is eternal.' Elliot said this several times to himself, slowly. Then he said, 'Well, yeah…of course that's true.'

I said, '…Yeah.'

We both lay back in our Posturepedic beds and smiled. I knew we were on the same cloud. He nodded off.

Gunther came in to check me out. He said his attempts to get those two 'rough studs' arrested and charged had grossly backfired. Not only was this one of those creepy rural communities that abided by its own rules; they were hosting a town fair in a month. They were expecting 'tourists' from neighboring counties, and didn't want the bad press. They didn't want 'no slut' hurting their economy, or trying to send their promising young lads to jail. We were practically chased out of town.

There was nowhere to go, so we headed back to Delilah's. I mean, we could have kept motoring, but we needed to regroup. Gunther and I, we're kind of shaken.

Delilah took the news with all the calm of a fucking banshee. She ranted and raved, punctuating nearly every sentence with 'What were you thinking?' directed at one or both of us.

Gunther said he didn't know I'd even left the room; he was out cold.

She said, 'Can't handle your liquor anymore.'

I said, 'I didn't know it would hurt so much.'

Delilah is clearly one of those people who shows they care by acting like everything's someone's fault. She stood out there on her patch of dirt, in the blazing sun, arms and tousled eccentric-person hair flapping frantically. I don't know how anyone can take themselves seriously with a name like Delilah. It'll be a long time before I head behind some shacks for some back door lovin' with a couple of hicks again. But this was just one of those unforeseeable mishaps.

She didn't think so at all. She said I'm young and should take care with myself; and others should take care with me, too. This was directed pointedly at Gunther, who looked like a dog caught peeing on the carpet. On a priceless Persian rug.

Gunther and I sat on the couch, drinking herbal tea. There were still a few door beads on the floor, here and there. He was sitting very close to me, with a heavy hand on my forearm, staring blankly at the floorboards. He's taking this a lot harder than I am. I just feel sore and kind of…stupid.

We had some dinner. Eggs on toast. I took a bath. Delilah hadn't wound down much. I decided to go to sleep. You could say it'd been a long day. Gunther came in and dropped the typewriter and some paper onto my cot. He still isn't saying much. He's a zombie, she's a banshee.

They were hollering at each other when I woke up. The sun was peeping through the tiny window, bright yellow. Everything was still tender. I got up to take a shower. There I was again, in the bathroom mirror. On top of everything else, I had beard rash. It didn't hurt or anything, just completed the picture. Man, I'm a damn seedy mess.

Those two were still yelling when I finally

ventured into the kitchen. They stopped and looked at me innocently. As if hushing up when I crossed the threshhold could conceal the fact they'd locked horns for the past half hour plus. The perfect crime. And damn it if it didn't look like they both had tears in their eyes. I bet no one got this upset when Gunther slutted himself around. But then, as far as I know, Gunther's never needed stitches in his ass.

Delilah flumped down on a kitchen chair across from Gunther (next to me), and said, 'Well, I'm going to do what I can. Not turning a blind eye.'

Gunther just blinked at her and sighed. Earlier I'd heard him yell, 'She's not your poster child, you maddening bitch!'

It seems Delilah is going to write an exposé on those guys, that town, the whole cover-up of a teenage rape and its witless victim. Apparently this is what I've been diminished to, by the words themselves.

Her editor loved it, of course. Who doesn't love kiddie porn? They wanted a picture of me but I said no. They named the town, fingered everyone. There was even a picture of the bar. Hell, there were pictures of the shacks behind the parking lot. They interviewed the ambulance driver, who described my wounds and their whereabouts. It couldn't have been more mortifying if they'd snapped a picture of me taking a dump and stuck it on a billboard. That's what I felt like doing to Delilah. She hadn't actually found the time to talk to me in the breakneck flurry of activity that surrounded the championing of my cause.

Gunther was still spitting mad. He burst into the living room early one afternoon and said, 'Are you feeling a little better?'

I said, 'Yes.'

He said, 'Good, because I'm getting you out of here.' He'd packed the car in a very haphazard, obviously hasty and irate fashion. He grabbed me by the wrist and deposited me in the passenger seat. He shut my door, and sped off in cloud of dirt.

We had to pass back through the offending piece of countryside to get to New York. I mean, pass much too close to that town for comfort. Gunther said we were only crossing the outer edge of the county.

I said, 'Gunther, I think we should go around.'

We were both kind of exhausted by this point, though. Nearing a destination, being able to stop, held a new appeal. So we stayed on track for now, and checked into a crappy motel just inside county lines. Or at least, we started to.

When we got up to the front desk, the clerk was reading the paper. When he saw us, he gave a snooty look of surprise, and mock pleasure. He snapped the paper up off the counter, completely concealing himself behind it, and continued reading it. This exposed us to the front page. It was us. I don't even know how they got a picture of us. We were driving, but it was still a pretty clear shot through the car window. The headline read, *Pedophile at Large*.

I scanned down the article. I couldn't take my eyes off it. It was too compelling. It would appear the good township had launched a counter-attack, alleging Gunther had kidnapped me and had been whisking me around the country having his wicked way with me since I was fourteen. (They didn't indulge in any punctuation, so why should I?)

Gunther turned on his heels. I followed him into the parking lot.

He said, 'I want to get out of here.'

I said, 'So do I.'

We drove half the night and ended up nowhere. We just slept in the car. The back seat was loaded up so we slept on the front seats, sitting up, holding hands.

I'm surprised I slept at all. But I did, and it was a pretty morning when I woke up. All soft blue sky, with wispy clouds, and birds singing in the trees. We were parked next to a weeping willow.

I told myself it couldn't be too bad. We'd be out of this layer of hell soon, this boil on the backside of the country. (Jeez, they were practically shaking pitchforks at us.) Surely not everyone had seen the paper. And of those that had, odds were high on most of them being illiterate.

We pulled into a doughnut shop for breakfast. No sooner had we got through the door than some freckle-faced hillbilly teen with shoulder length brown hair pointed at us and blurted, 'Hey. It's that guy. Dad, look—and that kidnapped girl.'

His dad turned on his stool slightly. 'Well, heck, so it is.' His ass crack was showing.

Gunther turned on his heels again. We sped outta there. We were half expecting them to make chase. In a pick-up truck. They shouted something as we left. I couldn't quite make it out; Gunther had already fired up the motor. I guess they had doughnuts to finish.

We found somewhere with a drive-through window and ordered some random crap, just to fill our tummies. I had fries with mine. And secret sauce.

Gunther drove and drove and drove, and didn't say anything. It started to get darker. We pulled up at a motel with an all-night diner attached. We'd traveled a long way today. Although it was still fresh, I wanted to think it was all behind us now.

We cleaned up and strolled into the diner. A woman with a blonde beehive hair-do and a cigarette hanging out of the corner of her mouth was seated at a booth, reading the paper.

And wouldn't you know it, there was a fucking picture of us. This one was smaller, and it wasn't on the front page. But sure enough, she raised her neon blue-shadowed eyes and narrowed them to a slit when she saw us.

'Oh Gott in Himmel,' muttered Gunther, with extreme exasperation. He doesn't speak German very often, but I kind of like it when he does. It's another vampirism about him. Most vampires started out on the Continent, I figure, and picked up a few languages over the centuries. 'Why choose this life now, though?' I thought to myself. It's not very glamorous. Or distinctive. And why wouldn't you just rise up and rip all these people's throats out?

'You know,' he said partly to me and mostly to the awful patterned carpet, 'I think I would just like to sit down and order a *fucking* meal.'

Gunther doesn't swear very often.

But he added, 'Fuck!' and strutted over to a booth on the far side of the room. The old bee-hived battleaxe said something to the waitress, who never came to our table. No menus, no 'Hi, what can I get ya?!' Not even a glance. No waters, no bottomless coffee.

Gunther said, 'What is it with these people?'

'People hate the P word, Gunther.'

We talked about driving around looking for an open supermarket or another drive-through fast food hole. We didn't feel like it in the end, and wound up getting potato chips and lemonade from a vending machine and going to our room. I noted internally that this was first time I had ever hit the vending machines with Gunther. Thus a new standard was set in vending machine companions, grumpy or not.

He said he wasn't going to scurry away like a fucking fugitive just because some fat blonde looked at him funny. So we sat in our room and smoked. And watched a James Bond movie. We both just stared at it. Those type of movies don't do anything for either of us, and my mind had plenty of chance to wander.

'Y'know, Gunther.' I leaned toward him. 'Some would say now we got nothing to lose.'

As I spoke, James Bond was gliding across a swanky hotel room to bed a vixen. Gunther blinked lazily at the screen. I was trying to cheer him up, give him some encouragement. But I had that little devil on my shoulder again, too. I can never tell if I'm a good person or not.

'Christ, girl,' Gunther muttered, finally. 'Your stitches—you're not even healed yet.'

'I mean later,' I said, 'I meant…' I was going to say 'love', but why bother mentioning that now? Even though by rights I could. To say that I love him is no overstatement. He rules my world; has me hypnotized in some sort of fevered love trance. I can't hold it all in, like a miser hugging all my riches to my chest, making sure none fall. I feel like it will all burst and go scattering. Like so many door beads.

I looked over at him. He looked tired.

Then he muttered with deadpan lethargy, 'Maybe when you're older.'

It surprised me to hear him say that. And it all

but confirmed my theory regarding his savoring his moment to freeze me into a love-locked eternity. Still, I can't believe he's putting me on the shelf. What the heck is wrong with starting your happiness now? What's wrong with loving someone who loves you; loving them forever? I think that's what everyone wants.

I smoked and typed on the old red machine for the rest of the evening, which pretty much brings us up to speed.

Someone wrote 'pervert' on our door; we noticed it as we left, very early in the morning. Only they misspelled it. What they had actually written was 'prevert'. I just incorporated it into my lingo. A couple times today I teased Gunther with something like, 'Why, Gunther, you old prevert.' He's been so down in the dumps lately, he barely cracked a smile. Maybe he's getting sick of my wisecracks. But I like to laugh, what can I say? If there's something to laugh at, I will. If that makes me immature, so be it. Glorie says it's good for your abdominal muscles, laughing.

We drove in complete silence, and I replayed

Gunther's blandly put but promising projection. There was the 'maybe', but there was also the 'when you're older'. How much older? I don't want to start losing my looks. Or my personality. People do say age gives you character. But for my money, most people, it just takes what character they have and pickles it into goo.

And, hang on a minute...maybe he's just trying to get me off his back. Like a parent. 'Maybe when you're older'—goddammit, it's not like I asked him for a puppy. This is love. He should give me a fucking straight answer. Leave me dangling...

I turned my head slowly sideways and gave him a contemplative squinty-eyed glare. He didn't see me. He was practically collapsed over the wheel. It was nearly check him for a pulse time. I wasn't about to get on his case about this latest quandary of mine, or anything else. No matter what happens, what's going on, when it comes to a future with Gunther, I still want to be in the running. So I try to behave myself.

It doesn't feel like we will ever escape this fucking hellhole of a county, which seems to be populated entirely by seething semi-literate pitchfork-wavers. It seems to be expanding as we try to reach its borders. Elliot, back at the hospital, had told me about a porno he'd seen at a party. Most unsexy porno, ever, he said. It was called Airtight, and consisted of a lady being fucked by several men trying to plug every hole they could think of. He said she didn't look like she was having much fun. So I guess a couple of local fellas trying to play Airtight with me behind some shacks was the most excitement this region has seen for a while. At least there were only two of them.

We got pulled over for a broken taillight, of all things. In broad daylight. The cop wrote Gunther up a ticket, told him to get the hell outta there, and spat when he said it.

Gunther suggested we stop only for gas; keep moving until we reach civilization again. I agreed.

It was at one of these gas stations that I did a scan of the magazine stand on my way to the ladies' room, and came across Delilah's article. I'd been wondering when that was coming out. I thought maybe at least it would clear up some of the nasty rumors floating around; clear Gunther's and my names. Or, at the very least, Gunther's. I didn't have to look far, either. It was staring me right in the face. The cover. Of a proper nationally syndicated rag. The headline: Little Girl Lost. Well now, that really boiled my potato.

I bought it, and showed it to Gunther. In the end, Delilah hadn't taken any pains to make Gunther and me appear above board. It was full of vague innuendo and half-assed disclaimers. ('Perhaps he *is* just a kind soul giving a waif a lift…')

Gunther rang her from a pay phone. He told her with sinister composure that if she didn't rectify this situation with a forthcoming truthful article, he was going to sue her for libel and assassination of character. Apparently she said she had already written that article, it was her editor who insisted on giving it that risqué slant. And she assured him she is as upset as he is.

He said, 'I doubt that very much.' And returned the handset slowly and heavily to the receiver.

When we got back to the car, he said, 'Maybe she'll get a fucking Pulitzer,' and threw the mag as far as he could. Which wasn't very far. But magazines aren't very aerodynamic, I guess. It landed all folded out and crinkled on the other side of the pumps. And then he just sped off. It's not like him to litter.

A few miles down the road he did something even more un-Gunther-like. He screeched the car to a halt, nearly in the ditch, got out, and just wandered off. Went trudging through the tall grass.

'Gunther?' I shouted behind him.

He mumbled, 'I'll be right back.' (I think.)

I thought maybe he was going to take a piss. After all, the world is one big men's room. However, Gunther always prefers to use proper facilities, so I doubted this theory. But I decided to give him some space anyway. He took ages though. I felt like it was getting darker. I got out and headed in the direction he had. He hadn't gone very far from the car, really. He was leaning against a weird sharp rock formation, smoking.

I said, 'Since when do you smoke during the day?' He lowered his eyes toward the joint and I took it from him. I didn't intend on smoking it. I just placed it lightly on my palm, like a little burning caterpillar.

'Gunther?' He didn't answer, and I hadn't thought of anything to say, anyway. My chest hurt, right through the middle. I took a drag of the joint. I took about five more, than handed it back to him. We made our way back to the car.

Then he just sat there, in the driver's seat. Sulking, I would say. I stared at him for a while. Then I said, 'Maybe we should keep driving.'

He said, 'Yeah…Can you?'

'Gunther!' I laughed, 'You know I can't drive…
Well…I can sort of…Do tractors count?'

'No.'

'Bumper cars?'

'No.' Now we were both smiling, a little.

He pulled off the road, onto a dirt road that was basically part of the prairie, nearly indistinguishable from the grasses growing up around it. He proceeded to teach me how to drive his old beast of car.

'About time you learned,' he said.

Seemed a strange time for a driving lesson.

'You're a natural,' he said.

'Been watching you.'

He chuckled, and kind of rolled his eyes.

There weren't many cars around, so after a couple of hours I ventured out onto the road. I was a little shaky, but I did OK. Gunther reckons I was speeding.

When we started nearing a town, Gunther took over the driving again. I'm not quite up to negotiating traffic yet. And all the stuff you have to do in towns; parking, stopping, starting, indicating. But I'm fine out on the open road.

Gunther checked us into a hotel. I stayed in the car. We brought everything up to the room. Gunther took a shower. I sat on the bed and typed up all the day's adventures: my driving lesson, Gunther's mysterious wander. It feels like we are finally out of the scope of the horrible vengeful hicks. Like we're back in the world again.

When he got out of the shower, I was watching Bambi on TV. He sat next to me on the bed and said, 'Oh, my small thing,' and I was reminded English isn't his first language. He stroked my hair. I nestled into his chest. He put his arms around me and held me for so long he fell asleep. I probably seemed asleep, too. But I couldn't sleep. Being close to him again was just too electric. I didn't want to miss out on any of it. So I stayed awake. Besides, I could hear his heart beating. So I just stayed up, listening to that, until I got too tired, and shuffled down onto my pillow. By then it was practically dawn. A bird was singing.

Gunther woke up and disentangled from me, efficiently but not without tenderness. He went through his morning routine to the letter. He was a little withdrawn still, but seemed basically composed. I really want him to get his old composure back. I find it reassuring. I don't like seeing him all frazzled. I don't know what to do. But he's a pretty sturdy old horse, I guess.

We went out for breakfast. I got pancakes. They were damn tasty, too. Big and fluffy, just like I like them. This place was a family-run restaurant. One of those ones with a slew of adorable kids serving you. A big lady who resembled Aretha Franklin waved at us from behind the counter with a wooden spoon. It was nice to be somewhere normal again. It didn't seem boring at all now. Normal seemed fantastic, sent waves of relief through me. They were all so nice to us, so friendly. I don't even care if it was put on. I'm not about to get picky. Our waitress even had pigtails.

As soon as we got out of town a ways, I took over the driving again. I really think I'm starting to get the hang of it. It's funny to look over and see Gunther in the passenger seat. He looks so helpless, just sitting not doing anything, not controlling anything. Well, not controlling the vehicle, at least. Truth be told, I don't glance over that way much. I really have to concentrate.

As we got further out into what felt like the middle of nowhere, I got my confidence up, and indulged in a lingering study of Gunther. He looked like road kill. Or maybe a particularly down-trodden hitcher. Looked like I'd just scraped him off the side of the road, exhausted and defeated. He was peering back at me with haunted eyes, filled with such desperation. I was overcome. A cat smile was spreading across my face. I wanted to squeeze him, but I stayed where I was. He said, 'That smile…that smile is…like a blanket.' He sounded like Brad Pitt in True Romance. He sounded stoned. Which wouldn't be anything out of the ordinary, except Gunther never acts stoned, even when he is. His diction is always perfect.

I stopped for gas and scanned the magazine stand for tales of the heartland. It looked like our story had stopped spreading. Hadn't felt like it ever would, felt like it would just keep growing like a wild fire. But it had thankfully been eclipsed by a genuine tragedy: a proper rape, a girl murdered. Her face was plastered everywhere. Our little incident was all but forgotten. When I got back to the car I tossed a magazine onto Gunther's lap and said, 'They're not interested in us anymore.'

He glanced down at the cover and droned, 'Stupid fucking world.'

I imagine it would be, if you'd lived through several different eras. I guess this one would look pretty ridiculous.

On the third day of me driving, he curled up in the backseat. He moved a bunch of stuff up to the front and stretched out as best he could. He said there'd been a change of course. We had been driving almost dead south. Now he directed me northeast.

I drove for a few hours with the radio on, eating corn chips. Gunther eventually poked his head up. I told him I was kind of tired, and asked if we could stop early today. He draped a hand heavily on my shoulder and said, 'You're not used to driving, I'm sorry.'

We agreed to stop in the next decent-sized town. His eyes looked weird. I put this down to a shortage of prey, a departure from his vital, secretive habits. He's been with me nearly all the time.

The approach to a 'decent-sized town' was heralded by a marked increase in doughnut signs. The number of pizza signs escalated, then fast food outlets of all description. We got stuck behind a funeral procession, making its way down the main street, then pulled into a motel.

We got to the check-in counter. We always pay up front. It was fifty dollars a night. Gunther took two wrinkled twenty dollar notes out and stared at them for a while. He held one in each palm, like he was comparing them. Then he said, 'Be a dear and pay the man, will you?'

I took each twenty from him, added a ten, and handed it to the clerk, who looked too bored to judge us. He was watching The Young and the Restless, and had a pink sweaty half-eaten burger sitting on his desk in a styrofoam container, which he was also using as an ashtray. Surely any distraction was a good distraction, but he seemed eager to get back to it; gave the distinct impression we were bothering him. Of course there were flies, buzzing around him in slow motion. They didn't seem to be bothering him. One even landed on his greasy forehead. He didn't bother to brush it off. I felt like swatting it for him. Felt like swatting him.

'Thanks,' I said.

'Um hmmm,' was his reply. He couldn't even manage an 'Enjoy your stay', but when I got to the room I could see that would have been a stupid thing to say. It was a musty shit hole. We may as well have slept in his burger container.

'Gunther,' I said, 'I'm so tired and hungry.'

'Yeah', he smiled, and we ventured out.

The funeral procession was still crawling along when we got onto Main Street. We were traveling in the opposite direction, so passed each creeping car. We were passing a metallic blue American rustbucket. The driver shouted, 'Well, what do you fuckin' know!'

It was Football Shirt. I said, 'Gunther, that's...' I didn't know how to put it, so I just said, 'That's the guy who crammed his dick in my ass.'

Gunther snapped out of his lethargy, or rather he incorporated the following actions into his lethargy, somehow: he glided smoothly over to the driver's door and with one graceful sweep of his arm, opened it and pulled Football Shirt out by his... football shirt. (Yes, he was wearing a football shirt to a funeral. But it looked like it had been pressed. And he was wearing what he probably considered dress jeans.) It was a shock to see this asshole again, full stop. We must have been a thousand miles from that fucking town. I was practically healed.

The guy in the passenger seat yelled, 'Hey, what the fuck!' and lunged across in a tardy attempt to play tug-of-war with Football Shirt. He jumped out and crossed to our side of the car, to the aid of his friend, who now had Gunther's knee in his balls.

I shouted, 'Gunther, no!' He was so clearly out-numbered. There were these two horrible creatures, and then there was the rest of the procession behind us, peeling out of their cars, rolling up their sleeves.

I've never known Gunther to resort to violence. I've only known him to string a lot of long words together. He was doing all right for himself, I must say. There was something very ninja-like about it all. I guess I could add martial arts to his bag of tricks. But I was too petrified to be impressed. These guys were trying to hurt Gunther. And they were encroaching on us like Dawn of the Dead zombies. Any second now, they would hurt Gunther, I just knew it.

Someone grabbed his hair, and pulled him backwards. I was on that guy in a second. I swung my leg up and kicked him in the balls. Like I say, I was nearly healed, and I only had one stitch anyway. But a high kick was ambitious, and I felt something tear. My jeans started filling with blood. Nothing major, just like I'd forgotten to insert a tampon.

Some of the people coming over were trying to stop the trouble. But most were joining in. I wanted to run away, but we were surrounded. So we just had to claw our way around this circle of hicks, like a couple of alley cats. Then a really hefty fellow arrived and put Gunther in a headlock.

You always picture yourself in situations like this and wonder what you'll do. I picked up something flimsy (a cardboard poster roll, I think) and I tapped him over the head with it. All it did was amuse him. When he turned around and smirked at me it made me so mad I picked up a free-standing traffic barricade and just about brained him.

He had a grotesque look of shock on his face, as he raised his hands to his head and looked for all practical purposes like he was trying to hold his brain in. Then he dropped to the ground and started to ooze blood onto the asphalt, B-horror movie style.

A shocked hush followed, which Gunther and I used as an opportunity to dart away. Some people looked up and shouted 'hey'. Some started to follow us, but we outran them. We ran in a big circle that led us back to the motel. We threw our stuff in the car and sped out of there, Gunther drove. Fuck the fifty dollars. We heard the scream of an ambulance. Three cop cars sped past us.

'God, Gunther,' I said, 'this is so twilight zone.'

He didn't say anything.

We drove a long way. And he was really speeding. I told him to slow down, or we'd attract attention. He slowed it down to the speed limit. We finally got to a caravan park. It was the middle of the night, and pitch black. I didn't know where we were, Gunther probably didn't either. He told me to stay in the car, and headed up to the reception cabin. He had to buzz for a while before someone came to check us in. She was an old lady in her bathrobe. Very matronly.

We were in the caravan when Gunther finally saw the blood on my jeans. He just stared at it, like it was a tarantula climbing up my leg, and he didn't know what to do.

Then he spluttered, 'Oh! Are you OK?'

'Yeah, I'm fine. Are you?'

'Uh, yeah. I'm fine, too.' Then he added, 'I think I broke my wrist.' After about twenty seconds he said, 'Hang on, I think it's just sprained,' and after twenty more, 'Are you sure you're OK?'

'I think so. I'm…I'm going to go take a shower.'

'OK.'

The shower was in a room that could barely contain it. And they'd managed to squeeze a sink and toilet in there, too. They were all on top of each other. The water pressure was what you'd expect from a caravan: a trickle, but I don't think I could have withstood anything stronger. Gunther came in and stood there, watching a thin trickle of watery pink run down my legs.

I said, 'Gunther, it's OK.'

He wandered back out again. I toweled myself off and joined him in the dank main section of the caravan. He was sitting on the bed, atop a stained orange plasticky bedspread. I curled up in my towel, facing the wall. He curled up next to me, and put his arms around me. Spoons, they call it. Eventually we got under the covers. I fell asleep and woke up with Gunther still clutching my naked body to him for dear life. His lips were on my shoulder. I could feel one of his fangs, just resting. If ever there was a time to bite me, this was it.

Once we were out in the daylight again, the feeling only got worse. I prayed he would bite me for real, not one of those flirty little nips. Gunther was driving. There was all manner of stuff littered about—fast-food billboards and people and cars and animals. My head was spinning, the world looked like a seething carnival. People were laughing, smoking cigarettes, and wearing bold patterned clothes, pushing strollers, chasing Frisbees, walking dogs, riding bikes, holding hands. It was all so bright in comparison to our darkness. I wanted to burrow. I wanted to dig a hole for us to hide. Hell, a grave.

I've started dreaming again, and remembering what I dream. Usually when I'm stoned I just get zonked right out and don't remember a thing. But last night I dreamed about the big funeral party brawl. Only this time, there was no funeral procession. There weren't even any cars. They were the zombies they appeared to be, swarming over the hills, converging on a single point, which was us. Zombie Football Shirt got there first. He was huge. He grunted. I said, 'Uh…small world.'

He said, mechanically, 'Not. Small. Enough.' Which didn't make much sense. It was very Arnold Schwarzenegger, though.

Gunther made the slow motion grab, as per real life.

The next zombie came up beside Football Shirt and said, 'Aw…He's. Just. Mad. Cuz. We. Broke. His. Toy.'

I remember thinking. 'Hey, they must mean me.' Then, 'I'm not a toy.'

As if he read my mind, Zombie #2 nodded

pointedly in the direction of my ass. I spun my head around. I had a wind-up string poking out of my butt.

'I say: head for the coast, one more friend, then New York City.' It was the new, slightly revived Gunther, driving again with proper gusto, with me on map detail.

I said, 'OK.'

I was still thinking about my dream. If only I'd slept a little longer. Maybe I could have found out what I say when someone pulls my string. But we got off to a very early start today.

We had burgers for breakfast. I guess you'd call that brunch. We sat across from each other at a tiny round plastic table, not saying much. But Gunther was looking at me steadily, with what I would classify as a beam, albeit muted. That sufficed, and well compensated for the lack of conversation. I was perfectly happy to sit there chewing, soaking up his silent approval.

He gave the waitress an extremely large tip, especially considering she looked and acted like oatmeal. She couldn't have been more unenthused, basically slapped the food onto the table, and slumped away. Slumped back over after a while, slapped something else onto the table. And when I asked for the bill she said, 'Pay at the counter,' listlessly.

When we'd finished I said, 'That was kind of crappy.'

Gunther flashed an amused smirk. 'Yeah, it was, huh?'

'I was hungry, though.'

'Yeah.'

We drove along for an hour or so listening to the radio. We'd found a classic rock station. In moderation, the classics make good driving music. That was certainly the case today. All sweeping farmscapes and 'Whole Lotta Love'. We stopped along the roadside to watch a horse being born. There was no one out there. Just a mare standing in the middle of a field, popping a foal out. As we happened to be passing. We stood there for ages, leaning on the fence, watching the tiny thing struggle to his feet, find the teat, follow his mother around on shaky little hooves. We could have been there for hours, for all I know. They walked over the crest of a hill and we got back in the car and drove away.

The seventies metal thing was still working for us. We drove along in comfortable musing silence. I don't know about him, but I imagine he was doing exactly what I was doing, and I was just letting those songs tell me what to think about. What to feel. What to imagine. A hawk was circling overhead. Over barns and wheat fields. Probably looking for field mice. It was almost quaint. It didn't quite fit the rock anthem sensibility, and all the thoughts that went with it. I thought of the vultures circling over stretches of barren desert, weird rock formations, and said, 'Gunther, I want to head out west again.'

'Spoken like a seasoned roadtripper,' he said.

'Yeah.'

We were quiet for a while. He was still driving east, of course.

I said, 'I'm just used to it now.'

'Not tired of drifting?'

I said, 'No.'

He said, 'You will be.'

It came to me in rush. The feeling is always just under the surface, so it didn't have far to travel…

'Gunther! What's wrong with me?' I grabbed his hand on the gear stick, and looked him square in the face.

He turned to me in confusion, surprise, and somehow managed to keep the car on course, despite continuing to hold my eyes. Which were pouring with tears. I was really sobbing now. I wanted this trip of ours to never end. And I wanted him to want it too.

'We'll go to Cynthia's,' he said, 'and get you a proper meal.'

It took him a while to finally come out with this. It was all he said about my outburst. It wasn't exactly what I was expecting. Or hoping for. But then, that's Gunther. Ever grounded.

We didn't make it to this Cynthia's house that night. We stopped at a seriously no-frills roadhouse well after dark and ate vending machine cupcakes for dinner. So much for getting a proper meal into me. I guess that would have to wait. Gunther was really letting his culinary standards slip. Three months ago he wouldn't have even considered those bite-sized snacks edible. He just wasn't putting the effort in anymore. I remember Murray witnessing one of our critical discussions, wherein Gunther was lecturing me about the finer qualities of something, the inferior qualities of something else. Murray, he of the cabin of rustic woodsy kitsch, told Gunther to stop patronizing me. I didn't see it that way at all. I like hearing Gunther tell me what's what. It always amuses me. And it always makes me feel as though he has bigger and better things

183

planned for me; like I have something important lying ahead.

I had another dream. I dreamed the whole journey, all the driving Gunther and I have done over the past several months, all our time together, could be traced on one huge diagram. According to this dream, if you were to hover above the country and look down, you'd see a gigantic organ covering almost the whole land, just flapped across it like a dead fish, gray and fleshy. It was criss-crossed by straps, tethering it to the ground. On the other end of some of these ropes and cords were Gunther's various friends, the recipients of our visits. I stopped hovering and plunged to earth; wandered around and collected their chatter, their accusations. Apparently this was Gunther's heart. The cords: our path across it, or across the country as it were. They are one and the same. I saw Stephanie a ways away. And Murray. Delilah got right in my face and said, 'We have to stop Gunther's heart from exploding.' I tried to digest this. She said, 'Haven't you ever heard of a heart attack?' I said, 'Yeah, but...' She turned and shouted, 'Hey, you guys! Kid's never heard of a heart attack!'

For some reason I was holding a needle and thread. Some dame I've never seen before came up beside Delilah and spat, 'The fuck were you gonna do with that?'

The next day we were at Cynthia's. She's this gorgeous blonde. One of the only friends of Gunther's time has been kind to. She opened the screen door and stood there looking like a goddamn siren, all statuesque and self-satisfied. I think her hair was actually blowing in the wind. And I didn't even feel a breeze. Like some film crew lackey was standing behind us pointing a fan. Like it was a goddamn photo shoot.

This imaginary wind seemed to have caught Gunther, too. He was standing next to me, towering and swaying like a poplar in a gale. He has been a little off color lately.

Cynthia took one look at him and said, 'Oh, Gun, no!' and grasped him squarely by the shoulders, as if he was in danger of keeling over. I'd never heard anyone use a nickname on Gunther. Except maybe Delilah. But let's face it, she's just a random word generator. Fucking journalists.

'Cynthia,' he said at length, 'I'm just…tired.'

'Uh…OK?' Her voice was laced with something; maybe sarcasm, I couldn't tell.

'And my young friend here is just hungry.'

She looked at me with mingled warmth and pity. And to Gunther she returned with a look of intense concern. Finally she turned on her heels and said flatly, 'Well then. Come in and have some rest and food.'

She wasn't expecting us. Gunther hadn't called. And it was kind of late. I didn't want her to go to any trouble, so all I ended up having was toast. Gunther didn't have anything. And she had a cigarette.

She got up and took my plate, and announced, 'Gun, you can crash with me. Bed's huge. Kiddie can take the couch.'

She got me some blankets and a fluffy pillow. She pointed to the remote and told me she had MTV if I wanted to watch it. I think I rolled my eyes. I wished a hundred wishes that Gunther would offer to take the couch; send me in with her. But he didn't. He trotted off obediently. God, who could blame him. She's just so smooth, there's no contradicting her. So Gunther was sharing a bed with another woman. A beautiful one, at that. And I lay essentially a few feet away, alone. I prepared myself to be visited that night by all manner of torment and anguish. But all I ended up feeling was a dull, throbbing numbness. I fell asleep, and awoke with a start, in a strange room with nothing but gray coming in the windows. I remembered something was wrong, and then remembered it was the fact that Gunther was in bed with someone who wasn't me.

Eventually we all got up, convened in the kitchen, and ate more toast. I wondered if Cynthia was one of Gunther's playmates from the heady days of hedonism. It wasn't hard to picture her in a drug soaked, leather-clad orgy. Then I wondered if she was a vampire. Talk about well preserved. Do vampires wear acid washed jeans? There's no need to be narrow minded, I guess. She was wearing a silk camisole.

She puffed out a big bluster of smoke and said, 'Kiddo, you are going to need more than just toast to survive.'

I thought that sounded kind of hospitable of her. But kind of foreboding as well. Cool, I thought. I wonder if my vampirization is nigh. Maybe those two had some kind of Meeting of the Undead last night to discuss my future development. Hopefully there was no sex involved. I'm starting to think I'm the jealous type.

Cynthia blew a few contemplative smoke rings and addressed me again. 'So I hear you're quite the existentialist.'

'Huh?' (Bearing in mind I'm not a morning person.)

'Gunther says you've read everything you can get your tiny little hands on.'

'Huh? Oh, yeah. I guess.' There followed a lame silence during which I took a sip of coffee, then another, and finally decided I should gratify her with a slightly meatier answer. 'Except Dostoevsky. I hate that prick.'

'Shit, doesn't everyone.' She snorted, and blew smoke out her nose.

She stubbed out her cigarette, in an overstuffed ceramic ashtray that bore all the trademark awkward lumps of a child's school project. But her house was utterly, undoubtedly childless.

She blurted, 'So Gun, you going to stay here until you get straightened up?'

This was all getting too cryptic for me.

'Gun' said, 'I am straight, Cynthia, I am…It's—'

She looked at him dubiously. He stammered on. 'It's been hard.'

I wanted to get up from my flowery cushioned

country-kitchen chair and wrap my arms around him. Us womenfolk studied him a while, from totally different angles, I'm sure. For one thing, she was standing up, looking down. I never look down on Gunther. He's right, it has been hard, especially these last few weeks; just out of control. Those watery blue eyes looked like they had clouds in them, like he was dreaming of Heaven, of floating away.

I took a shower, and Cynthia turned her attention back to me. I came out in an oversized shirt, with dripping limp hair.

'That just won't do,' she said. I was marched back into the bathroom. We stood there side by side in what turned into a full-scale makeover. She put her own face on, and handed me recommended products intermittently. She lost patience with my haphazard application, and took over the entire exercise. She held my jaw in her slender hand, with its perfect red fingernails. My lips were painted. She told me to close my eyes, and did the upper lids. I was told to look up, and my lashes got a coat of thick starlet fake-eye-lash-style mascara.

'You have perfect features,' she said, matter of factly, almost bored. 'I mean, take them separately.

That's a perfect nose. Perfect lips. Perfect eyes.'

She seemed like a straight-up kind of gal. 'Cynthia?'

'Yeah?'

'What's wrong with me?'

She stopped looking like a high-class whore. The veneer fell away. She stood just behind me, gazing at me in the mirror. She smoothed my hair, from the scalp all the way down to the tips. She had one of those adult The World is a Shitty Old Place looks on her face. She dropped her hands to her sides.

'Gunther?' I could tell this was rhetorical, and couldn't form an answer anyway. Does a dog want the biscuit you're holding in your hand?

'Beautiful girl.' I thought she was going to leave it at that, she was quiet for so long after she said it.

'You want him…Want to be like him?'

'Yeah.' And I added, 'I am like him.' Then wavered modestly, '…Becoming like him…I think.'

'Yeah, well,' the five-star-hooker bravado was creeping back, 'to be like him, you'd have to not want him anymore.'

She may as well have sprinkled pixie dust all around me. The room seemed to be going white. I felt like closing my eyes. Time passed, and I don't know how much of it. She looked a little smug for my tastes. I finally recovered with, 'How zen.'

'C'mon Princess,' she said, 'let's go unveil you to the old critter.' I'm not a princess, and I hate being called one. I couldn't make any sense of this broad. Besides, Gunther doesn't need to see me all dolled up to get the notion I'm pretty. He's seen me with no clothes on.

Gunther was on the couch. He raised his eyebrows when he saw me. Cynthia trotted me toward him like I was on a catwalk.

He smiled, and scoffed, 'That's one way to disguise natural beauty.'

I felt myself blushing. And smiling. I didn't know whether to be happy or embarrassed. Happy, I guess. Because the make-up I could wash off. The beauty was there for, well, a while anyway.

'I *slaved* over this face, Gun,' Cynthia said, with mock pathos.

'No need,' he said.

'Look at you, you old slob,' she said tartly. 'I think the kid and I should stage an intervention.'

He looked well annoyed, and said in a lazy, bitter monotone, 'Leave the innocent out of this.'

'The Innocent'; Gunther-speak, if ever I've

heard it. You can see why I think he's a few hundred years old. Has anyone spoken this way for the past couple of centuries? I did wish Cynthia would get off his back about whatever the heck it was she was on his back about. She should be happy she's sharing a bed with the guy. I should be so lucky. I wondered if there was cuddling, a light fang on the shoulder. I doubt it. Maybe that's what all this is about.

And I can't believe he still considers me innocent after all I've gone through lately. I sat next to him. Cynthia turned on the TV, and was standing too close to it to hear us.

'Gunther. I'm not really that innocent anymore.'

He looked at me with a steady sorrow. His eye looked moist. I thought I was going to have to get him a tissue. But then I remembered he always carries a folded handkerchief. We were sitting real close together, and just looked at each other for a while like that. Cynthia left the room.

He said, 'You're a baby.' Sometimes it makes me mad when people say stuff like that. But he said it with such affection and conviction. For a second I felt protected, felt precious. As only he can make me feel. And then it swiftly dawned on me how much distance that verdict places between us, and I wanted to rid him of the notion so badly I thought I might cry, which would have been a pretty unconvincing rebuttal.

So I sat fuming, cursing the irony: every experience I've racked up that I consider a step closer to Gunther makes everyone, including him, treat me that much more like a fucking child. No one treated them like children when they cavorted around playing promiscuous hippies…They all pretty much scored lifetime memberships in the Promiscuous Hippy Club.

I know things now…I know what things feel like. I belong in his club, if anyone does. I stole a look at Gunther. He was giving me that downcast look that is becoming all too familiar, basically the look that's haunted his face off and on since I staggered behind a shed with a couple of rough hicks. But I'm still the same person I was before they laid their big stupid paws on me, when he looked at me with 'love in his face' and not this distant, useless pity.

I really did burst into tears then, and snapped, 'I'm not some broken toy, you know.' For lack of any recent physical contact, I smacked him on the arm. 'I'm not a fucking broken toy! You can't just, don't just…' I was breathing too hard. I stopped shouting, and sort of gasped, 'Can't just throw me away.'

He held me until I stopped crying. He said no one was throwing me away. And he said, 'Sorry, so sorry,' just as he'd said to Stephanie. But he sounded like he really, really meant it.

Cynthia came back, smelling of fresh nail polish. She had on 'The MTV', as she calls it, and was holding her fingers splayed out at her sides, swaying to some godawful loud song. Some nouveau punk. Gunther and I hate that shit. I saw him cringe ever so slightly, and it made me feel somewhat better, made me feel like we were still on the same side.

We walked her to work. She runs a secondhand retro clothing store. You wouldn't know it to look at her. Gunther wanted to go to the library. I went back and forth between the animal and art sections, mostly looking at pictures. Gunther was scanning all the periodicals. We were there for about an hour. When we were walking down the steps, back out into the sunny day, he said, 'He's all right.'

'Huh?'

'That guy you clobbered over the head.'

'Oh, him.'

'He's going to be OK.'

'That's good.' I probably should have sounded more enthused.

'That *is* good. Now you can't be charged with second-degree murder.'

'Hmmmph.'

'Yeah, hmmph.' He clapped a hand on my shoulder.

We walked down the street and got some ice cream in the diner. Meandered over to the shop. We brought Cynthia a soda. She was very appreciative. I tried on about a million outfits. She gave me a shirt. It's kind of a green seventies number that hugs my waist. Cynthia said it makes me look like Stevie Nicks. Kind of an odd compliment, I think. Gunther approved.

That night I lay on the couch and watched MTV. Couldn't sleep. They had on a Blondie retrospective. Now there was a beautiful woman, the old Debbie Harry. I've never known anyone to disagree with that statement. Seems she's *everyone's* type. I decided I should try and get some sleep, and switched it off. That's when I heard the moaning.

I pricked up my ears, hoping I was mistaken. But there was no mistaking it. Cynthia was carrying on like a porn star, all thunderstruck gasps. I couldn't believe they were fucking. After all that fussing and not getting along. But then, I guess that's always the way. You can be as patient as a saint with a man, and he just goes for the first hardened bitch to slap him with some criticism. Some good old nagging. Seen it a million times. And heard plenty a nice girl complain about it. My friend Jemma, in high school, caught her boyfriend cheating on her with her dykey aunt, who ran the tuckshop at juvenile hall. And Jemma used to iron his shirts. In high school.

That fucking moaning just went on. I felt like getting up and hovering in the doorway, floating over the bed like a vengeful ghost. Because you do wish you could just be dead, in moments like these. Just make it all stop. Finally it did, with simultaneous moans from both of them.

Gunther was up early the next day. He walked past me, slouching, and didn't meet my gaze. What am I, the wife?

He muttered, 'Good morning.'

I replied, 'Fuck's sake.'

He said, 'I'm sorry?'

And I said, 'Nothing.'

Cynthia had no problem meeting my eyes, brash bitch. She was strutting around the place like she had bluebirds on her shoulders chirping out happy songs. Seemed she hadn't had a good lay in a long time.

But it wasn't enough of an occasion to fix anything other than fucking toast. Again. So much for going to Cynthia's and getting a good meal into me.

I took a shower and fumed over this situation. There was no way in hell I was going to hang around while those two fucked each other. That was just too much to bear.

I wrapped myself in a towel and stormed down the hall, dripping. Gunther was coming the other way, and grabbed my upper arm, gently.

'We'll leave today,' he said.

I kept walking, and dressed so quickly I got all my clothes wet. I sat on the couch with the intention of watching more MTV, but was so wet I could feel a puddle forming under me. And they were playing booty-shakin' RnB. This whole scene was getting more and more pathetic. Too lame even to serve as a symbolic reflection of my current downtrodden spirits. So I went outside and sat myself on the porch in the sun, to dry.

Gunther passed me with some bags. He'd packed my bags, too. I heard the jingle of car keys, from inside the house.

And I heard Cynthia say, 'That's it? C'mon, Gunther!'

She got on the phone to another friend of theirs. Told Gunther to stay until he got here. Murray, as it turned out. Took him half a day to get here. Old walrus face.

I was on the front porch smoking a joint all to myself when he pulled up. He was jovial as ever when he saw me. He shouted, 'Hey, you little hooligan!' and smooshed me in a long bear hug. I'm pretty sure I accidentally singed a hole in his flannel shirt.

Gunther came out to meet him, and Cynthia stood in the doorway. Murray released me and turned his attention to Gunther, with a 'Hey, old buddy', and punched him on the shoulder.

He went inside with those two and said, 'Still make quite the handsome couple.'

I stayed out on the porch. This situation really was trying my patience. I heard them talking inside, but couldn't hear what they were saying. And I wasn't really listening. This is Gunther's and my trip. We decide when we come and go. In fact, mostly Gunther decides. And that's fine. Because he's Gunther.

It was like watching a cheetah get hit by a tranquilizer dart. It was just unnatural, undignified. Unholy. In the name of friendship, in the name of old flames, in the name of whatever the fuck, I wished they'd just release him. And I couldn't believe he didn't have the balls to stand up to them, but yet he'll stand up to me, who'll walk to the ends of the earth for him with smoking embers on my toes. Couldn't believe he was kow-towing to these peripheral fuckheads. I mean, they go back a ways, but what about now? It's me. It's me and him. And we need to get back to it. And I wish he'd make it happen, the way he makes everything happen. And I was well stoned.

I got up, stood in the doorway, and said, 'Gunther?'

He looked at me with all his gentleness.

And Cynthia looked at me at the same time and said, 'Little lady, you're out of your depth here.'

'Don't underestimate the kid, Cyn.' It was Murray who stuck up for me, while Gunther just stared at me weakly.

'We're not leaving tonight, are we?' I addressed this to whoever had the wherewithal to answer. No one spoke, and Gunther looked at me with an expression of even more weakness. So I said, 'I'm going to go sleep in the car.'

Cynthia said, 'You can take my bed.'

I was already on my way out the front door when I said, 'No fucking way.' As if I would lie down in their crusty love juices. I wasn't going to sleep in any bed in which Gunther had so recently bedded someone else. God fucking damn it.

Strange, because Gunther is Mr. Protocol, but when I got to the car, the keys were in it. I guess Cynthia really startled him into submission. They were lying on the driver's seat. What did I have to lose? The man I love was in the talons of someone else, and we needed to get out of there, even if it was only one at a time. *I* needed to get out of there. I just couldn't stay one minute longer. I needed to show Gunther. They can't stop us. They can't stop me.

Before I knew it I was hurtling down the black rocky road, bouncing over the jagged little country-road stones, under the towering pine trees. It was kind of spooky. But also kind of exhilarating. And it seemed the perfect way to show Gunther what a lame ass he's being. Show him how it's fucking done. And show him what it feels like to be without me. Let him wonder when I'll be back, for a change. But then I thought, 'When will I be back?' Was I even going back, or was he supposed to come after me? I just knew I wanted to get moving. Beyond that,

I didn't know what I was doing. The concept of heading out on my own and calling the shots was cool. But it only meant something if Gunther could see it. Could feel it. I don't like to kid myself.

Do I really need him here, though? I can feel him from everywhere. Such is love. Maybe I could leave him, after all the trouble he's caused me, and feel my leaving him, for a long, long time. Feel him, wherever he is, knowing he's done me wrong, and I am at large, punishing him. In all my innocence.

I slept in the car, pulled over in a ditch. I woke up the next morning when Murray's pick-up pulled up alongside me. Turns out I'd only driven a few miles. I got sleepy. And truth be told, I don't think I really wanted *that* much distance between me and Gunther. He was sitting in the passenger seat.

He leaned out the window and said, 'Had us a little worried.'

It was about 4:00 or 5:00 a.m. The sun wasn't even up yet. He disembarked from the pick-up and came and sat next to me. I turned us around and drove back to Cynthia's house. I think I got my point across.

We left later that day, amidst loads of hugs and affirmations. God, for a jaded gal, Cynthia really could lay it on thick. And Murray, he was always pretty affectionate.

After a long silence and safe distance, I said, 'That was weird.'

Gunther said, 'Yeah. Don't worry about that.'

We drove half a day, and stopped at a roadhouse, where I finally got a decent fucking meal. With onion rings. And finished off with apple pie. A mug of coffee. And some lemonade. Gunther got a conservative grilled cheese and tomato sandwich. On Wonderbread, which he pulled apart and looked at with disdain. He had two coffees and a tall glass of water.

It was getting late, and we planned on driving some more. So we found a little corner shop, and got some supplies. When we walked in, there were a couple boys around my age playing pinball. One of them stopped dead when he saw me, dropped his hands to sides, and his jaw, and blurted, 'Gawd DAMN!' He nudged the other one.

I don't think my entrance really warranted that. (And oddly, I thought I saw Gunther blush.) I think if anything, I was looking a little worse for wear. Sleeping in the car hadn't done me any favors.

I never knew this country was 85% hick towns,

until this trip. Up until driving around the whole damn thing with Gunther, I was happily ignorant of the fact. And now we were in the South. Again. I don't know how that happened. Gunther was driving.

He got some change and used the pay phone outside. He stayed on a while. It sounded important, but I don't like to pry.

There was an altercation between two large men when we were walking back to the car, in the parking lot. I don't know the origins of the dispute, but as we came upon them one said to the other, '…Why you bitch-faced asshole.'

To which the other replied, 'Did you just call me a…*bitch-faced asshole?*'

I was glad we were down South, because it didn't seem right to ask that sort of question without a Southern accent.

Gunther grabbed my arm and said, 'Come on sugar, let's get out of here.' And herded me 'round towards the car.

'Did you just call me…*sugar?*' I laughed. Now even Gunther was going Southern. 'Jeez, why don't you just call me molasses?'

He was quiet.

'Gunther, huh?'

He snickered.

We really sped along after that point. We drove all night. Gunther had a bunch of coffees, and manned the wheel. I slept in the car, for the second night in a row.

And would you believe when I woke up the next morning, I saw the monstrous constructions of New York City, towering in the distance.

'GUNTHER!' It was as much an accusation, as a plea, as a jolt of shocked surprise.

'There it is,' he said, matter of factly.

So here it looked like Gunther, the knight in shining armor, had delivered me to safety after all.

I couldn't believe it was all over. And, not one to beat around the bush, I turned to him and gasped, 'Gunther, is it all over?'

He paused, and said, 'It's only just beginning. For you. Small One, it is only the beginning.'

Tears poured down my face. That damn huge city just appeared out of nowhere.

Although once we got into its midst, into those narrow cluttered streets, with the buildings that climbed up to the sky…all that mayhem was distracting. I got lost in just looking at it all. I had

204

more tears, but it was as if they forgot to fall.

We drove around, and around, and around until Gunther found somewhere to park. He took me on a walking tour of Lower Manhattan, which comprised the East Village, the West Village, SoHo and the Lower East Side. We even contemplated walking across the bridge to Brooklyn. Oh, and Little Italy, and China Town. It's all pretty close together, really. At least, it seems close together, because you don't know how far you're walking, because there's so much to look at.

We paused on the corner of Houston and Ludlow, where that gross Katz's Deli belches out the combined smell of pig fat and sweat. Heaven help anyone walking past those air vents. He reached out and stroked my hair. Usually he's a bit cagey about that sort of thing. But I guess old guys probably stroke young girls' hair all the time in Manhattan. I don't know why he doesn't just stay on. Seems like no one would bat an eye here. But then, I guess Gunther is just Gunther, wherever you put him. An island. Damn, though, I'm still hanging on to the hope he might not go.

We found the car again and headed over to Glorie's house, which was uptown a ways. This is where I was to be deposited. It took us fifteen minutes to find a parking spot. A taxi driver gave us the finger. Glorie came to the door in a pant suit and just stood there for a minute, looking at us. She looked more ordinary, less theatrical, without her clouds of smoke rising around her old body like vapors. Seeing her there squinting in the harsh sun on her doorstep, I was reminded of an old roadhouse bar at closing time, when a flash of fluorescent lights kills all the shadows; you realize the perceived ambience was a lie. But then she took a long filtered smoke in one hand, a dinged-up bejeweled lighter in the other, lit up, inhaled, exhaled, air kissed us, and waved us inside, as the old Glorie, the Glorie I remembered. She took my wrist and pulled me into this ornate bear cave of hers; I felt I didn't quite belong here, but was way too curious to turn back. I wondered how many times Gunther had visited, and what he'd done, what memories of his rest here among piles of papers, sketches, huge potted plants, peacock feathers, bookshelves packed to the ceiling, strolling cats, cobwebs, old carved couches, empty bird cages, the sound of wings flapping overhead. I trotted along behind her with Gunther at my heels, properly awe-struck. This place actually has pillars. Inside. It's palatial. If ever there was a head vampire, she is it. Vases, statues, paintings, a goddamn fountain, all as elegant as the hostess herself.

She had a room made up for me, complete with a teddy bear on the pillow. I guess she thought I needed a little TLC. There is a little too much pink in this room for my taste, but I really shouldn't complain. All in all, this Glorie is a class act. She's not a headcase like Gunther's other friends.

Gunther stayed the night, in his own room, of course. But he did stop by my room with a huge stack of high quality recycled typing paper. I made him promise to come and say goodbye to me in the morning. He did, and I sat up in bed and hugged him and cried. He cried too, but maybe just because tears can be contagious. I got up out of bed and watched him walking through the pillars. I heard him at the front door, thanking Glorie. His name was pounding in my head. 'Gunther. Gunther!' I felt like screaming it like Stanley screamed 'Stella' in A Streetcar Named Desire.

I spent the morning with Glorie, drinking tea and catching up. She certainly is well read. And well versed on a damn lot of things. What I guess you would call an interesting conversationalist. She pointed me toward a good bookstore. I went for a walk, and said I'd check it out. But I didn't, I just kept walking. Past the flashing billboards of Times Square, through the gray streets in shadow, with their mannequined windows and hurtling commuters. South, until I got to the grittier sections of town, where the streets could talk to me.

I passed a wall of graffiti that said:

I am avenging absences
I AM AVENGING ABSENCES
I need someone as wounded as myself

I'm not sure how I came to be here, alone and insignificant. Most people my age walk around in gaggles of twittering friends. Or so it seems. I don't even want that. Can't remember if I ever had it. Or how I came to be by myself. I guess there is no one reason. It's a collection of things.

I waited on the corner of Bond Street, on the Bowery, for a truck to pass. It spluttered out smoke. It looked like the trail of its breath on a cold day. Right then it didn't seem to matter if I waited for this big animated truck to pass, or walked in front of it. I do just feel like wandering out into the traffic, there's no denying that. Sometimes I get so tired of all the stuff cluttering up my brain, it's a relief to feel I could be reduced to so many pounds of raw, jiggling flesh that could just go thud and stop.

Alphabet City was just as Gunther and I had left it. Full of junkies, walking with their sinking, measured steps, as if they were leaving tracks in the snow. So peaceful, so divine. I wanted to follow one and learn his secret.

I sent another message to Gunther. 'Gunther,' I thought, 'it's not what you've got for me, it's what I've got for you.' Because I have all this love left over, and nowhere to put it.

And he decided not to bite me after all. Silly Gunther. Pointless Gunther. Now I'll just have to find someone who will.

Acknowledgments

I would like to thank everyone at Text Publishing and Picador UK for believing in my first book, and shepherding it into the world. For sharing the joy and nervous anticipation inherent in this process, Krissy Kneen. I would also like to acknowledge the support of the Queensland Writers Centre, and independent bookshops, with special thanks to my locals: Avid Reader and Riverbend Books. *The Ice Age* was chosen for the Pathways to Publication Masterclass at Varuna, The Writers' House. I'm grateful to everyone I encountered there, including my fellow authors; most notably Angela Meyer, for her undying enthusiasm for literature from all corners, and Amy Jackson, for tolerating a frequently distracted writing partner, and for nudging *The Ice Age* in the direction of Text Publishing! Thanks of course to Peter Bishop, for everything he does for emerging writers, and for being the first person to love this book, and make me feel like an author.

picador.com

blog
videos
interviews
extracts